Secret Agent, Secret Father

DONNA YOUNG

MILLS & BOON®

First published in Great Britain 2010
Large Print edition 2010
Harlequin Mills & Boon Limited,
Eton House, 18-24 Paradise Road,
Richmond, Surrey TW9 1SR

© Donna Young 2008
ISBN: 978 0 263 21591 5

Harlequin Mills & Boon policy is to use papers that are natural, renewable and recyclable products and made from wood grown in sustainable forests. The logging and manufacturing process conform to the legal environmental regulations of the country of origin.

Printed and bound in Great Britain
by CPI Antony Rowe, Chippenham, Wiltshire

DONNA YOUNG

an incurable romantic, lives in
beautiful Northern California with
her husband and two children.

To Wendy and Jimmy,
I love you, Mom and Dad!

Chapter One

With the pain came consciousness.

It pierced the cataleptic depths with jagged teeth that gnawed through skull and skin.

The man lifted his head, testing. Blood coated his tongue, coppery and thick. He groaned as the nausea tightened his gut, pressed into his chest.

They're coming! The words screamed at him through the blanket of fog, adding a bite to the pain. His eyes fluttered open. Blurred lines altered, then cleared into comprehensible patterns.

Rain trickled in through the half-shattered windshield. The splatter of water mixed with his blood turning the air bag pink in the semi-darkness. A light pole lay bent across the top of the sports coupé, its base uprooted from the cement.

How long had he been unconscious? He shifted, trying to relieve the pressing weight on his lungs, focusing on the half-deflated air bag wedged between the steering wheel and his chest.

A shaft of white heat impaled his right shoulder. He let out a slow hiss.

After a moment, he pulled his other arm in from the driver's side window, noting for the first time he held a pistol tight in his grip. The silver flashed in the night. The cold steel felt good in the palm of his hand. No, more than good, he thought. Familiar.

He fumbled with the safety belt, released the

lock. Tightening his jaw, he shoved his good shoulder against the car door, stiffened at the new surge of pain, the wave of dizziness. Metal scraped, glass crackled. Another push and the door gave way. Slowly he slid through the opening and then stood, using the mangled roof for support.

Sirens wailed in the distance. Instinctively he turned. Bile rose, burned his throat. The ground tilted beneath him. Swearing, he fell to his knees and vomited.

They were coming for him. Cops. Rescue workers. It didn't matter which. Both filed reports.

Reports left paper trails.

With gun in hand, he waited a moment for his stomach to settle, using the time to get his bearings.

Rows of houses, dull with age and earth-toned brick, flanked the street. Each with covered porches that lay behind picket fences or scattered hedges. Each containing onlookers, mostly white-haired couples, their arms tightly wrapped over their chests, holding closed a variety of plaid and terry cloth robes.

Those who didn't brave the elements took protection from the rain behind the narrow bay windows of their homes. Their fingers held the curtains slightly apart, while eyes squinted with curiosity and fear, deepened the grooves of their features.

Enough fear to keep them away from the armed stranger who had invaded their quiet suburban neighborhood.

Carefully, he turned his head, his eyes searching the shadows of the road. How far was he from her?

A bent street post lay no more than five feet from the wrecked light pole. Proctor Avenue?

Too far, his mind whispered. Too far to help.

The sirens grew louder placing his rescuers no more than a few minutes out.

Hot needles pricked his eye sockets and images began to swim. A black fog seeped in, setting off another wave of dizziness. Struggling against the void, he rammed his injured shoulder into the car. Pain exploded through his arm, jarring his spine, driving consciousness forward, forcing the obscurity back.

Sheer willpower put him on his feet. He swayed, then stumbled. *Warn her,* his mind screamed. Before he passed out. Before his enemies found him.

Or worse, the whisper came. *Before they found her.*

Chapter Two

A storm swept over the outskirts of Annapolis. The air crackled and snapped, alive with the hum of lightning, the boom of thunder. Below, stinging sheets of rain pounded water and land with heavy fists, spurred by the fierce Chesapeake winds.

Grace Renne stood by her bay window holding one billowing curtain in her grip. When the bark of the storm reached her, a twinge of sadness worked up the back of her throat.

For the last several years she'd lived on the

bay, admiring the city's fortitude, appreciating its history. It was a city born amidst the turmoil of the American Revolution. Time-honored traditions cemented every cobblestone, forged every piece of iron, framed every structure for more than three hundred years.

Grace caught a whiff of burning wood—fireplaces combating the early autumn chill. Underneath the smoke lingered the richer scent of the sea and sand. Slowly, she drew in a deeper breath, enjoyed the bite of salt on the back of her tongue.

She loosened her grip until the curtain fluttered against her fingertips. Scents, textures… intuition were her tools to live by. Characteristics, her father insisted with irritation, she'd gotten from her mother.

She'd gotten her mother's looks, too. The pale, blond hair that hung in a long, straight curtain. The light brown eyes that softened with humor, narrowed in temper. Delicate features—until one looked close enough and saw the purpose, the character that shaped the high cheekbones and the feminine jaw.

She shut the window, smiling as Mother Nature beat at the framed glass. Any other time, any other mood, she would have let the storm have its way. Her eyes swept over the oak trim of her cottage, the barreled ceiling, the endless stacks of half-packed boxes. But the cottage was no longer hers, sold only days before to her friend and bar manager, Lawrence "Pusher" Davis. The reformed ex-con had bought her home as his first step to becoming a real-estate mogul. And she was sure he wouldn't appreciate water damage on his new hardwood floors.

"We won't have nor'easters in Arizona, baby," she murmured and patted her stomach, a habit begun to soothe the first trimester bouts of nausea.

And now? Grace stopped midmotion. What did her father say? A subconscious attempt to soothe a restless spirit?

Better than no spirit, she'd countered and brushed off the ache just beneath her heart.

With the window shut, the air grew thick with the sweet scent of baking cookies. A grin tugged at the corners of her mouth. "I'd say, handsome, that patting you is a self-defense mechanism to divert your constant cravings for warm milk and chocolate chip cookies."

Her oversized, navy sweatshirt fell to midthigh—its Annapolis insignia covered her midriff like a big yellow target. The shirt, combined with the thick cotton of her dark leggings, provided more than enough warmth to allow her to go barefooted.

Still, she threw another log onto the fireplace's burning embers. Its muted glow matched her melancholy mood.

Overstuffed furniture of glossy, dark oak and warm tweeds filled the room. She hadn't packed up the rich, brown chenille throws that draped the back of the couch. Putting it off had been a silly defiance, she thought. But even as she did, her hand ran over the nearest throw, her fingers curled reflexively into its thickness. After five years, she wasn't quite ready to give up the first true home she'd ever known.

The buzz of the oven timer broke through her thoughts, but the growl of her stomach prodded her into the kitchen. Tiles of white and corn-flower-blue checked the six-foot counter—effectively separating the kitchen from the main room without diminishing the cottage's warmth.

For once, Charles Renne had agreed with her decision to move. In fact, her father encouraged her. Surprising, since he hadn't agreed with any of her choices in years. She'd been fourteen when her mother had died. But the war of wills had started long before.

She snapped off the oven and opened the door. The heat blasted her in the face. She hesitated over a long, drawn-out and downright decadent sniff.

The small flutter in her belly told her she'd gotten the baby's attention. She laughed, low and easy. "Okay, sport, one plate of cookies and glass of milk coming up." With an expertise born from cravings, she took the cookies from the oven and slid them onto a nearby cooling rack.

Lately, her battles with her father had flared to a whole new level. One that heightened after her refusal to reveal the baby's father.

The baby was hers. Only hers, she thought stubbornly.

That characteristic she inherited from her

father. But it hadn't made the past pleasant for either father or daughter.

Four years ago, she'd stopped by a cigar bar called The Tens to meet a group of college friends.

The pungent smell of whiskey and the more earthy scent of imported cigars drew her in, but it was the low murmur of conversations and clink of glasses—a backbeat to the smoky jazz—that seduced her.

Two weeks later, she dropped out of premed and bought the bar with the rest of her trust fund. An emancipation of sorts, she thought in hindsight.

For the past several years, she'd indulged her passion for fast cars and jazz clubs and leaned ever more closely toward liberal ideas. And the more she indulged, the more distant her father grew. The more distant he grew, the more she hurt.

But over time, the freedom she'd gained became precious and the pain bearable.

The doorbell rang, startling her. She glanced at the mantel clock.

Almost midnight.

Unease caught at the base of her spine. She pushed it away, annoyed. "Who is it?" she asked, but heard no response. Only the wind whistling through the crack beneath, tickling her toes. She curled them against the floor. A look through the peephole proved useless.

"Hide." The command came low, splintered. Still, she recognized the underlining timbre, the slightly offbeat drawl that turned one syllable into two.

"Jacob?" She yanked open the door. He sat next to the door pane, his back propped against the side of the cottage. Blood coated him from top to chin, dripping off the slant of his jaw onto his torn shirt and his black dress slacks. "Oh my God. Jacob!" She fell to her knees beside him.

His eyes fluttered open, focused for a brief moment, one black pupil dilated to more than twice the size of its partner. Blood rimmed the iris until no white could be seen. "Hide, Grace." He rasped the order. "Before they kill you."

His head lolled back. Fear gripped her. Quickly, she placed her hand under his shirt. *Please, God.* The rhythmic beat of his heart remained steady beneath her palm. She closed her eyes briefly against the sting of tears.

The rain and wind spit at them. She raised his hand to her cheek, felt the ice-cold fingers against her skin. She glanced around and saw no car. How had he gotten here? Walked?

Her nearest neighbor was down the beach, too far to call for help. If she left him outside, he'd be worse off by the time the ambulance got there.

A few weeks ago, the doctor had said no heavy lifting. What would he say if he knew the father of the baby lay half-dead on her porch?

"Jacob!" She screamed his name, but he didn't stir.

She scrambled inside and grabbed her purse from the counter. She'd call the ambulance from the front porch—

Then she heard it, the familiar ring tone of her cell phone.

She dumped the contents of her handbag onto the counter, ignoring the lipstick and keys that fell to the floor. She snagged her phone, saw the displayed name and punched the button.

"Pusher?" She flipped the overhead switches on. Lights flooded the room, making her blink. A glance to the doorway told her

Jacob hadn't moved. She ran back to his side, checked the pulse at his neck.

"Grace? Thank God." Pusher Davis paused on a shaky breath. "Are you okay?"

"I'm fine but I need you to—"

"Then you haven't talked to anyone?"

"Talked…" she said, momentarily off balance. Using the cuff of her sweatshirt she wiped the blood from Jacob's forehead, trying to get a good look at the injury beneath. "Pusher, I don't have time for this." His skin grayed in the porch light. She had enough experience to know he'd lost too much blood. "I need you to—"

"Helene's dead."

"Helene?" Tension fisted in her chest. "Dead?"

"Grace, I found her body outside The Tens. In the back alley."

Helene, dead? The fist tightened, catching

her breath on a short choke of surprise. It couldn't be true. She'd just seen Helene earlier that day. They'd met at their favorite sidewalk bistro for a farewell lunch.

"It's Monday night. The bar should've been closed. She shouldn't have even been there this late. What happened?" The question slipped from her lips, but a prick at the nape of her neck told her the answer.

"She'd been shot," Pusher answered, then paused. "Grace, last time I saw her she was with Jacob Lomax."

She studied the wound in Jacob's shoulder, forced herself to inhale. *Hide, Grace, before they kill you.*

"Did you hear me?"

"Yes," she answered, then took another breath to steady herself. "Are the police there?"

"Not yet. But I've called them."

"Pusher, listen to me." She nearly screamed

the words. "I need you to stall them when they get there. They're going to want to talk to me, but I can't right now."

"I don't think you understand, Grace. Helene has been murdered—"

"I understand." She cut him off, not trying to stop the urgency of her words. "Jacob Lomax collapsed on my porch a few minutes ago. He's been shot, too," she added, deciding to put her trust in Pusher. "And until I find out why, the police will only complicate things."

"But if Lomax is there—"

"I told you, he is."

"Then why the cloak-and-dagger, Grace? If Jacob has been shot, this could have been a robbery. A simple case of wrong place, wrong time. I've seen it before."

"I don't think it is and I need some time to make sure."

"Why? Do you think he shot Helene?" He

said the words almost jokingly. But when she didn't respond, he swore. "You do, don't you?"

"No," she snapped. "I think his life is in danger."

When the manager didn't say anything, she added. "I can't explain right now. And I can't do this without your help, Pusher. Please," she whispered.

"Okay, okay. Lord knows, I owe you," he answered, the uncertainty thickening his Texas drawl. "I can probably stall them until morning. A little longer if they get ahold of my rap sheet. Will that work?"

She could trust Pusher to take care of the police. The ex-con had certainly sold her on hiring him a few years back, against Helene and her father's wishes.

"Yes, that will work," she said. "Thanks, Pusher."

"It's been a while since I've been in an interrogation room. Was feeling a little homesick, anyway," he mused before his tone turned serious. "Grace, watch your back. The cops aren't your only worry. I won't ask again why you think Jacob's in danger. But if you're right and he is a target, you could become collateral damage."

"I'll be careful."

She hung up the phone. Calling an ambulance was out of the question now. Not until she found out what was going on. She glanced at Jacob before hitting the speed dial.

The phone clicked on the fourth ring. "Hello."

"Dad, it's Grace."

"Grace. Do you realize what time—"

"Dad, I need your help." Jacob's wound couldn't wait for her father's lecture. "Your medical help."

Suddenly, his tone turned sharp. "Is something the matter? Is it the baby?"

"The baby?" She gripped the phone tighter. Deceit warred with desperation inside of her. "Yes, it's the baby."

"Are you spotting again?"

"No," she answered, not wanting to add that possibility to her father's worry. "But I can't explain over the phone. I need you to come over here now. And don't tell anyone where you are going. I want to keep this private."

"Don't tell… Grace Ann, maybe you had better explain—"

"Not now, Dad. Please," she added to soften her order. She moved her hand over Jacob's heart, took reassurance in its steady beat against her palm. "And bring your medical bag."

"I will, but I want to know what's going on when I get there."

"I promise full disclosure," she agreed. "And Dad, do one more thing for me?"

"What?"

"Hurry," she whispered.

Charles Renne hesitated for only a split second. They might not understand each other's views, but he was a father. One that understood fear. "I will."

Grace snapped the phone shut and shoved it into her sweatshirt pocket. Her father would take a good hour to reach her from Washington, D.C. Jacob couldn't wait that long.

"I can do this but you need to be easy with our baby, okay big guy?" It took some shifting, but she managed to maneuver herself behind him. Rain soaked her sweatshirt, plastered her hair to her forehead. Impatiently, she brushed the blond strands away, then slid her hands under his arms and around his chest.

Jacob was a good six inches over her own five-eight frame, and had well over fifty pounds on her. He was built lean, with the firm muscles and long limbs of a distance runner. Grateful her taste didn't run toward male bulk, she settled him back until he rested against her chest and shoulder.

The clatter of metal ricocheted in the night air. She glanced down. A pistol lay on the cement, its barrel inches from her feet.

His? Once again, her mind rejected the idea that Jacob had shot Helene. No matter what secrets he carried, he wasn't capable of murder. From the moment Helene had introduced Jacob to Grace, there was no doubt about the close friendship between the two.

Ignoring the weapon, she gripped him between her thighs. Slowly, she scooted him back through the doorway. Using the strength of her legs and arms, she tugged and pulled in short bursts of energy. The struggle took more than twenty minutes. Twenty minutes in which she pleaded, prayed, begged and swore. But she managed it.

Once inside, she scooted back toward the fireplace and lowered his shoulders gently to the floor. Quickly, she closed the door, grabbed a pillow and placed it under his head.

For months, she'd worried about him, raged at him—yearned, grieved, loved him—silently through the long, dark nights.

But not once had she been terrified for him. Until now.

His face was pale, stark against his deep brown hair, now darker with rain, sticky with blood. His features cut in razor-thin angles. Sharper, leaner since the last time she'd seen him. A four-inch gash split the hairline above the middle of his forehead. Blood and bruises covered most of his features.

She knelt beside him, saw him shiver. Cursing herself, she threw a few more logs on the fire.

But it was his shoulder that worried her the most. Blood was everywhere. His face, neck and arm were coated with it. From his head, or shoulder, or both. She couldn't be sure which.

Her pulse thickened with fear, making her hands heavy, her fingers tremble. She shook them, trying to settle them and her nerves, then removed his suit jacket. A shoulder holster crowded under his arm. Something she hadn't noticed when dragging him in. Quickly, she unbelted the holster and tossed it aside. Within minutes, she had him stripped to his underwear and covered him to the waist with her comforter.

The bullet had torn a hole through his right shoulder, leaving an exit wound on the back side.

Fear and confusion warred within, but right now she had time for neither. Instead, she crossed to the linen cupboard and pulled out a clean, white hand towel.

After running the cloth under warm water,

she returned to his side with it and her biggest pan filled with hotter water. She tucked the blanket around him, knowing she couldn't do anything other than clean the wound until her father got there.

With gentle fingers, she brushed a lock of hair from his forehead, then systematically dabbed the blood away from the gash.

"I'll give you one thing, Lomax," she whispered. She rinsed the towel out in the water, watched it turn pink, before she switched her attention to his shoulder. "You sure as hell know how to make an entrance."

Chapter Three

"He's coming, Mr. Kragen."

Oliver Kragen sat on a park bench as dawn broke over the Chesapeake Bay. His enforcer, Frank Sweeney, stood no more then ten feet away, his bulky frame eclipsing the sun behind him. Dressed in an Armani suit, the man appeared more like a pro football player ready to renegotiate his contract than the mercenary he was.

And that's exactly why Oliver had hired him.

"I'll give you odds the bastard screwed up."

Oliver didn't acknowledge Sweeney's comment. Instead, he waited until the click of shoe soles sounded behind him. Rather than turn in greeting, Oliver tossed the remainder of his Danish to a nearby pigeon. After all, Boyd Webber wasn't a peer, he was an employee.

"She's dead."

Oliver glanced at Sweeney, a silent order to leave. Once the big man stepped away, Kragen spoke up, but his focus remained on the pigeons at their feet. "How?" The question was low, pleasant.

Boyd wasn't fooled. But he didn't care, either. The ex-marine had more than two dozen kills under his belt and had survived more horrors than the bloodiest special effects ever created. Nothing on this earth made him afraid of dying. Least of all a weasel like Kragen. "The Garrett woman had a gun. They both did. It forced my hand."

"They forced your hand because they were armed? They're government operatives. What did you expect, Webber?" Kragen's voice hardened. "If I remember right, I told you it was imperative that the Garrett woman was to be brought to me. Alive."

"It was a mistake. They killed one of my men, wounded another. The third man targeted Lomax, but somehow the woman took a stray bullet in the chest."

"And this third man?"

"I killed him."

"To save me the trouble? Or him the pain?"

"I was…angry." More than angry. Infuriated. Enough to lose his cool and shoot until the woman was dead. Enough to murder another man—one of his own—who had witnessed his transgression. "My man should have been more careful," he lied.

In Webber's opinion, Helene Garrett

deserved no better than to die in a gutter. She had betrayed Senator D'Agostini. Slept with him, used him, stolen from him. End of her, end of story. Or it should have been. But the files were still missing.

"Did you clean up your mess?" Kragen's eyes shifted to his coffee cup. He took a sip, burned his tongue and swore.

"I thought it better to leave things." Resentment slithered down Webber's back, coiled deep within his belly. He studied Kragen's profile with derision. Kragen was the poster-boy politician. The meticulous, trimmed blond hair that enhanced the high slant of the cheekbones, the aristocratic forehead. A nose so straight that Webber would bet his last dime that Kragen had it cosmetically carved. All packaged in a five-figure topcoat and custom suit. All done to hide the trailer-park genes that ran through Poster Boy's veins.

"You killed your man without consulting me first." Oliver glanced up then. Twin metallic-gray eyes pinned, then dismissed the mercenary in one flicker.

"I consulted with the senator beforehand," Webber responded.

Oliver noted the verbal jab, but chose to ignore it for the moment. "Did you search the bar? Her apartment?"

"She'd moved out of her apartment days ago and left nothing behind. And we had no time to search the bar. Lomax was the priority."

"The woman had the files and the code," Oliver insisted. "I want the bar searched. And I want Lomax found."

"Shouldn't take long. We winged Lomax before he slipped away. We found his car wrapped around a light pole."

"Did you follow the blood?"

"Witnesses told the police he took off down

the street but the rain washed away any bloody trail."

"And the police? What do they say?" Oliver prompted, his annoyance buried under a tone of civility. More than the Neanderthal deserved, in Oliver's opinion.

To say that Webber was ugly would have been polite. He had the face of a boxer, flat and scarred from too many alley fights, and a bulbous nose from too much booze. Like Sweeney, he wore a tailored suit, had no neck and too much muscle. Unlike Sweeney, he sported a butch cut so close it left the color of his hair in question.

"The police are questioning the bar manager. An ex-con by the name of Pusher Davis."

"If the man is an ex-con, they'll suspect him first," Oliver observed. "Tail him, just to be sure. I don't want any loose ends."

"There won't be. The police won't get

anywhere. Helene Garrett will become just another statistic in a long line of unsolved homicides," Boyd explained.

For the moment, Oliver ignored the arrogance underlying Webber's words. "They have Lomax's blood on the scene."

Webber snorted. "Won't do them any good if they have no records to match it with. Right now, the cops don't have any information on either of them. Or the senator's connection to her."

Webber was right. Oliver had gone to great lengths to keep the senator's relationship with Helene Garrett private. A precaution he practiced with all the senator's mistresses. "That won't get us the Primoris files or the code. We need to find Lomax."

"My men are checking nearby hospitals and clinics."

"You actually expect him to show up on

some grid? He's injured, not stupid, Webber," he snapped, annoyed over the fact that this wouldn't have happened if Helene hadn't slipped under their radar.

Oliver had investigated Helene months before the senator had started the affair. With his contacts, it took Oliver no more than a few calls to get everything from her finances to her elementary school records. False records, as it turned out.

"From the look of his car seat, he's lost a lot of blood. If he passed out, he'd have no choice. Someone might have taken him to the hospital."

"Find him."

"It would help if you could give me more than just his name."

"I gave you his name *and* the time and place of the meeting." Oliver paused, his eyes critical. "It should have been enough."

"I told you, they forced my hand. It couldn't be helped."

"Just find Lomax and keep him alive. I don't care what it takes," Oliver ordered, already making plans to advise the senator to call an emergency meeting. The others would have to be informed. "That bitch stole the Primoris file. I want it back. Do you understand?"

"I'll take care of it," Boyd responded automatically. "And the police?"

"I'll make a few calls. Jacob Lomax won't be on their data banks unless I arrange to put him there."

"Are you thinking of making the murder public?" Webber questioned.

"No." Any unwanted attention at this stage could sabotage their plans. "At least not for now." Not until the others met and reevaluated the situation. They were too close to their goal.

"How about her partner?" Webber asked. "Grace Renne?"

Oliver considered the possibility. "She might know something. Or at the very least, have seen something." Oliver remembered faces, names. It was vital in his world. He'd met Miss Renne once at some sort of political function—one of many. At the time, the association between Helene and Doctor Charles Renne's daughter seemed coincidental—and, in his mind, added to Helene's credibility. But now...

"They had lunch yesterday afternoon," Webber prompted.

"Then you should have already had someone talking to her this morning." Oliver stood, his gaze back on the horizon. He didn't like disloyalty within his ranks. And those who were foolish enough to betray him suffered. "I'm here in Washington, D.C., with the senator until after the fund-raising ball tomorrow night. You know how to get hold of me. And I mean me, Webber. The senator is too busy with the upcoming election to be bothered with this. Do you understand?"

Not waiting for an answer, Oliver turned to Sweeney. "Frank." He waited the moment it took for the enforcer to join them. "You're with Webber. Make sure he does his job this time."

"Now wait a minute—"

"Yes, sir." Sweeney stepped behind the mercenary, boxing the man in between Kragen and himself.

"One more thing." Oliver grabbed Webber's wrist. When Webber automatically jerked back, Sweeney clamped down on his shoulder, holding him in place with a viselike grip.

"I want to make sure they don't force your hand this time." Slowly, Oliver poured the cup of coffee into Webber's palm. Within moments, the hot liquid raised blisters. "Be diplomatic, Webber," he cautioned with noncommittal coolness.

Webber nodded, his jaw tightened against the pain until the skin turned white under his ruddy complexion. "And if the Renne woman doesn't want to cooperate?"

Oliver dropped the mercenary's wrist and tossed the cup to the ground. "Then be discreet."

Chapter Four

He wasn't dead. It took a moment for the thought to seep through. Another for the layers of fog to dissipate.

He surfaced gradually, registering the extent of his injuries. The throbbing at his temple, the ache over his brow. When his right arm refused to move when commanded, he shifted his shoulders no more than an inch. Pain rifled through him, setting off waves of nausea that rocked his belly, slapped at the back of his throat.

But his heart beat.

For a full minute, he concentrated on the rhythmic thumping, worked on breathing oxygen in and out of his lungs.

A keen sense of danger vibrated through him. But when his mind searched for details, he found nothing but the urge for caution. And an underlying edge of danger.

Slowly, he opened his eyes. The ceiling beams doubled, then danced before finally coming into focus. His gaze slid from the white ceiling to the white bandage on his shoulder.

With his good hand, he carefully searched the bed around him but found nothing. He let his arm fall back to his side. Molten heat blasted through his upper body, setting his shoulder and ribs on fire and telling him he'd been carelessly quick with the motion.

Cloth brushed leather, drawing his attention. Slowly, he turned his head. No more than four feet away, a woman straightened in the leather wingback chair. She uncurled her long legs in one slow, fluid movement. The morning light washed over her in soft pink rays, coating both her skin and pale blond hair in a hazy blush.

"You're awake." Her sleep-soaked voice reminded him of crushed velvet, rich and warm. But it was caramel-brown eyes that caught his attention. Carmel dusted with gold, he realized as she drew closer.

And edged with concern. Enough to tell him she'd spent the night in the chair.

"Is the pain bearable?" Her face was scrubbed clean, revealing a few freckles dotting her nose. With long, blond hair tied back into a ponytail and clad in jeans and a black, zipped hoodie two sizes too big, she looked no older than a first-year college student.

The back of her hand drifted over his cheek.

Her cool, soft touch soothing. So much so that he felt a curious ache in his chest when it dropped away.

"No fever, thank goodness. How are you feeling?"

He caught her wrist with his good hand and jerked her closer. It was a mistake.

Skin pulled against stitching, bones ground against cartilage. A curse burst from his lips in a long, angry hiss.

"Where is it?" His question was barely a whisper. Dried bile coated his tongue in a thick paste, leaving his throat sandpaper-dry.

"Where is what?" she demanded. But a quick glance at his shoulder kept her from tugging back. He didn't have to look because he felt it. Blood—thick and warm—seeped from his wound into the bandage, dampening the gauze against his skin.

"The 9 mm. Where is it?" he repeated, pushing his advantage. Whoever she was, she wasn't smart to let him see her concern.

"In the nightstand drawer. Both the gun and the two clips." Her temper surfaced, sharpening her tone.

He didn't take her word for it. Instead, he reached down with his bad arm—grunting at the shock of pain—then opened the drawer with his fingers.

But his actions took effort. Sweat beaded his forehead, his arm shook against her when he grabbed the pistol.

"Let go of my wrist." The fact she kept her words soft didn't diminish the anger behind them.

Or the concern.

Immediately, his hand dropped to the bed. More from weakness than her demand, he knew.

"Trust me, if I wanted you dead, I wouldn't

have saved your butt last night." She rubbed her wrist.

Jacob resisted nodding, not wanting to set off another wave of dizziness. But he tightened his grip on his pistol. "What am I doing here?" His voice was no more than a croak.

She poured him a glass of water from a pitcher on the bedside stand and offered it to him. "Recovering."

When he didn't sit up, she lifted the glass to his lips. The cool water hit the back of his throat, immediately soothing the raw, burning heat. After he finished, she placed it back on the nightstand.

"What happened?" he murmured, resting his head back against the pillow. The room tilted a little. That and the water made him queasy.

"You have a gunshot wound in your right shoulder, a forehead laceration and a concussion. You were lucky the bullet only caused minimal damage. We've stitched your wounds, but only rest will help the concussion," she explained, her voice softening once again with concern on the last few words.

First he digested her reaction, then her explanation. A bullet hole meant he'd lost a lot of blood. A hindrance, but not debilitating. "Who is we?"

"My father." She hesitated over the words, enough to obstruct any natural warmth in them. "He'll be back in a moment."

"How did I get shot?"

"I was hoping you could tell me."

The sunlight grew brighter, casting beams across the bed. When he grimaced, she crossed the room and pulled the curtains shut.

"And you are?"

She stopped midmotion, her eyes narrowing as they pinned him to the bed. "If you're trying to be funny, I suggest you work on your timing. Because whatever sense of humor I might have had, you destroyed it about five months ago."

What the hell was that supposed to mean? "Trust me, the only joke here is on me." His laugh was no more than a savage burst of air. "So why don't you tell me who you are and we'll go from there."

"Grace. Grace Renne."

Grace. He took in the serene features, the refined curves of her face that sloped into a slightly upturned nose, a dimpled chin and a mouth too wide to be considered movie-star perfect. But full enough to tempt a man, even a half-dead one like himself, to taste.

"You don't recognize me?" she asked. Disbelief—no, he corrected, distrust—lay under her question.

So she didn't trust him? Seemed fair enough, since he didn't trust her.

"Should I?" Vague images flickered, their edges too slippery to grasp. He focused beyond the disorientation, the fear that slithered from the dark void.

Again, he found nothing.

"Yes." She turned back to the curtain, took a moment to tuck the edges together until the sun disappeared. "We were friends. Once."

Her voice trailed in a husky murmur. A familiar bite caught him at the back of the spine. He swore under his breath.

"Once. We're not friends now?" He wasn't in the mood for cryptic answers or a prod from his libido. Obviously, his body needed no memories to react to its baser needs.

Sledgehammers beat at his temples, splitting his skull from ear to ear. He used the pain to block out her appeal.

"I'd like to think so," she responded. "What do you remember?"

"Not sure." Admitting he remembered nothing was out of the question. Clumsily, he shoved the thick, plaid comforter off him. Immediately the cool air took the heat and itch from his skin. She'd stripped him to his boxer briefs, he realized. Bruises tattooed most of his chest and stomach in dark hues of purple and brown.

He tried again, searching his mind until the headache drove him back to the woman for answers. "A bullet didn't do all this damage," he remarked even as the void bore down on him with a suffocating darkness. He took a deep breath to clear his head, paid for it with a sharp slice of pain through his ribs.

"Feels like I've been hit by a train." Anger antagonized the helplessness, but something deeper, more innate, forced a whisper of caution through his mind.

"Someone tried to kill you last night." She

spoke the words quickly, as if simple speed would blur the ugliness of them. "They almost succeeded."

Frustrated, he swung his legs over to the side of the bed before she could stop him. He fought through the vertigo and nausea. But the effort left him shaking.

"Where are my pants?" If he needed to move quickly, he didn't want to be naked doing it.

"You don't need them right now. You have a concussion." She glanced toward the door. "You need bed rest."

"What I need is my pants." He glanced up at her, saw the anxiety that tightened her lips, knit her brow. But once again, it was the fear dimming the light brown of her eyes that bothered him. He hardened himself against it.

The woman was definitely on edge. He tried a different tack. "Now," he ordered.

For a moment, he was tempted to raise the gun, point it at her, but something inside stopped him.

As if she read his mind, she glanced from the weapon to his face, then surprised him by shaking her head. "You won't shoot me over a pair of pants."

"Don't bet on it," he growled. Right now, for two cents, he'd put a bullet through his own forehead just to relieve the pounding behind it.

"Then go ahead," she said before she swung around, leaving her back exposed. The movement cost her, he could see it in the rigid spine, the set of her shoulders. He'd scared the hell out of her but she didn't give an inch.

"Damn it." She had guts for calling his bluff, he gave her that. "All right, it seems I'm more civilized than I thought."

When she faced him, she didn't gloat.

She had smarts, too, he thought sarcastically.

He placed the gun on the nightstand beside him and ran his free hand over his face, ignoring the whiskers that scraped at his palm. "Look, for the time being, I'll accept the fact that you and I are…friends. But whoever did do this to me is still out there somewhere. And I assume they'll try again. Agreed?"

"Yes," she replied, if somewhat reluctantly.

"If I have to face them with no memory and very little strength, I'd at least like to have my pants on when I do it."

"Your pants and shirt were covered in blood. I burned them in the fireplace."

When he raised an eyebrow, she let out an exasperated breath. "Fine. There is a change of clothes for you in my closet."

She waved a hand toward the double doors beside a connecting bathroom. Another good idea, considering the state of his bladder.

But he'd be damned if he'd ask for help. He'd

wait a moment for his legs to stop shaking. "Do I usually keep clothes in your closet?" he asked, knowing the answer would explain the pinch of desire he felt moments ago.

"You forgot them here," Grace explained and glanced toward the open bedroom door.

"And here is?"

"Annapolis." She paused for a moment, the small knit on her brow deepened. But when she brushed a stray hair from her cheek, the slight tremble of her fingers gave away her nervousness. She tucked her hands in her pockets. "You really don't remember, do you?"

"Right now, I don't even know what the hell my name is."

"Jacob Lomax."

He searched his mind for recognition. Found nothing that was familiar. His headache worsened, making it difficult to think. "How long have I been unconscious?"

"Since midnight last night." She glanced at the alarm clock on the nightstand. "Ten hours."

"Which makes today, what?"

"Tuesday. The twenty-third of September."

Slowly, he scanned the room, searching. The curtains and comforter, while a yellow plaid, were both trimmed with white lace. The latter was draped over a pine-slotted sleigh bed that sat more than three feet off the floor. Positioned across the room were its matching dresser and mirror.

Jacob studied his image. The blade-sharp cheekbones, the strong, not-quite-square jaw, covered with no more than a day's worth of whiskers. He rubbed his knuckles against the stubble on one cheek, hollowed more from fatigue he imagined than from pain. A bruise dominated the high forehead, spilled over in a tinge of purple by the deep set eyes of vivid blue.

No flashes of recognition. No threads of familiarity. Nothing more than the image of a stranger staring back.

His focus shifted down. Assorted lotions and powders cluttered the top of the dresser, along with a few scattered papers and a stack of books.

Packing boxes sat opened on the floor. Some were full, others half-empty, but most lay flat, their sides collapsed.

"You're moving?"

"Yes—"

"You're awake." A man entered the room, the black bag in his hand and the stethoscope around his neck identifying him as a doctor.

Grace met the older man halfway across the room. Jacob deliberately said nothing and waited. But his hand shifted closer to the gun beside him.

Her father was on the smaller side of sixty, with a leanness that came with time on a tennis court, not a golf course. His hair was white and well groomed, combed back from a furrowed brow.

After a few murmured words, he patted her shoulder, then approached the bed. "Jacob, my name is Doctor Renne. Grace tells me you don't remember what happened."

"That's right." Since the older man didn't ask Jacob if he remembered him, Jacob assumed they'd never met.

"How's the headache?" Doctor Renne pulled a penlight from his pocket and clicked it on. He shined the light in Jacob's eyes. First one, then the other. The bright flash set off another series of sledgehammers. He winced. "Bearable."

"Look up…now down." Another flash, another jolt of pain.

"How did I get here?"

"Since there was no car, we assumed you walked. Grace discovered you on her porch last night." The doctor clicked the light off and tucked it back into his inside pocket. "Stay focused on my finger without turning your head."

Jacob followed the doctor's finger, this time ignoring the pull of discomfort behind his eyes.

"There's definite improvement." The doctor waved his daughter over to the bed. "Grace, I'll need your help. I want to check his shoulder."

They eased Jacob back against the headboard. The doctor examined the bandage. "There's blood. You're moving around too much. I didn't spend hours stitching you up for you to take it apart in five minutes."

"Thanks, Doc. I'll remember that," Jacob commented wryly. "I'd tell you where to send the bill if I knew where I lived."

"Your driver's license says Los Angeles, California," Charles answered. "Seems you're a long way from home."

Home? Why did the address, even the word, sound so foreign?

Grace leaned over to adjust his pillow. A light floral scent drifted toward him. For a moment he tried to identify the flower, but came up with nothing. Still the fragrance was distinctive. Feminine. Clean.

"Do you remember a woman named Helene Garrett?" Grace asked without looking up.

Frames of shadow and light passed through Jacob's mind, but nothing he could zero in on, nothing to bring into focus. "No, but…" Suddenly, a snapshot—vivid but brief— flashed across his mind. A woman laughing. Her cheeks and nose pink from the falling snow. Her smile wide, her eyes brimming with…happiness?

No, he realized suddenly. Not happiness. Love.

Chapter Five

"You." Jacob nodded slightly toward Grace, then frowned. "I see you."

"From last night or this morning?" The doctor asked, then took Jacob's wrist and checked the younger man's pulse against his watch.

"From a ski trip." Jacob closed his eyes, for a moment, trying to bring the image back. "I remember her hovering over me." When he opened them again, he caught the surprise in the doctor's features.

The doctor didn't know about me. Jacob

decided not to mention how the scent of her shampoo triggered the memory. Not until he understood more.

"You were skiing? Where?"

Grace nearly groaned aloud at her father's questions. When she'd found out she was pregnant, she'd told him the father of the baby was no one he knew. Just someone she'd met skiing.

Lifting her chin, she met her father's glare head-on. "In Aspen. A few times."

When her father said nothing, her gaze shifted from him to Jacob. But her smile was forced, her teeth on edge. "You fell the first time we were there." What she didn't add is that he had faked the fall, pulled her into the snow and spent the next twenty minutes kissing her breathless.

She hugged her arms to her chest and walked over to the window.

She didn't want to see the anger—the disappointment—emanating from her father.

"Who's Helene Garrett?" Jacob's question snapped the thread of tension between father and daughter.

"A business associate of yours. And my partner. Ex-partner. She introduced us," Grace admitted reluctantly, but she continued to stare out the window. The bay's waves crashed against the sand and dock, not quite over its temper from the night before. She'd stayed awake all night helping her dad, jumping at every sound the wind and rain made. But no one came after her. No one pounded on the door or jumped from the shadows.

Hide, Grace. Before they kill you. The words floated through her mind for the thousandth time. But was the threat real or a side effect to his amnesia?

"Someone shot and killed Helene last night

outside our bar." Grace could feel Jacob's eyes on her, studying her like some specimen in a jar. Something he'd done while they dated. Before his habit unnerved her, now it just annoyed her.

Amnesia. Her nerves endings snapped and crackled. She didn't believe him at first, but that lasted only a few moments. Admittedly, she had expected Jacob to clear up the confusion—the fear—that plagued her all night. How can you fight your enemies when you have no idea who they are? Or hadn't known they even existed until only hours before?

"And you assume because I took a bullet, I was there, too," Jacob said coolly.

He wasn't asking a question, but her father answered anyway. "It's a logical assumption."

"Did Helene have a gun on her?" Jacob asked, his tone flat.

"Yes, but you didn't shoot her. And she didn't

put that bullet in your shoulder, either. The two of you were very close," Grace insisted, but she didn't face him. Not yet. Not when her emotions could be seen in her expression. The doubt, the fear. Everything in her being told her he wouldn't harm Helene. She had to believe that, for now. "You might not remember who you are, but I know what kind of man you are. And you aren't a murderer."

"Well, for all our sakes, I hope you're right," Jacob replied grimly.

"I am." Her chin lifted, defiant; she was under control again. She was betting her life on it. More importantly, their child's life. "How long do you think his memory loss will last, Dad?"

The doctor had remained quiet. She swung around, challenging. "Dad?"

"I can't give you a definitive answer, Grace. We're dealing with the brain. Anything can happen. The concussion, while it's nothing to dismiss, doesn't appear serious enough to have caused permanent damage. Of course, I would prefer to order him to undergo some tests and a day or more of observation to be sure." The words came out rigid, censured. "Without them, I believe we're dealing with more of a dissociative amnesia. A loss of memory due to a shock rather than an injury to the brain."

"Traumatic as in Helene's murder," Jacob replied. "So this is mental rather than physical."

"In my opinion, yes," Charles answered, but he prodded Jacob's head wound, checking it. "If that's the case, my guess is that your memory will return in bits and pieces over the course of time." Her father took off his stethoscope and placed it in his bag.

"What span of time?"

"There is no telling how much will come back or how long it will take."

"He remembered his gun," Grace commented. "First thing when he woke up."

Dr. Renne glanced at Jacob, surprised. "You did?"

"Yes." He flexed his right hand, spreading his fingers. "I know I've been trained to use it. Even if I don't remember the when and the why." The confidence reverberated deep within him, hollow echoes from an empty void.

"That explains the other marks you're sporting. Two bullet scars on your back and a six-inch knife scar on your hip."

Charles Renne moved from the bed, his bag in hand. "Some traits—like combat training or studied languages—will surface instinctively. But most memories are triggered by emotions, reactions, physical evidence. A scent. A song. Any number of things. Experiencing them might eventually help your recollection, but there are no guarantees."

"He also remembered my name. Last night, before he passed out, he called me by my name," Grace inserted.

"If that's true, why don't I remember you now?" Jacob asked.

"Something must have happened while you were unconscious. Your brain could've just shut down from the emotional shock," Charles said. "If that's the case, your mind will decide if and when it's ready to remember."

"If?"

"There's always the chance you might not regain any of your memories," Charles indicated. "Especially those from last night."

Jacob considered the doctor's words. The sense of danger intensified after the mention of Helene Garrett. Could he have killed a woman he considered a friend? There was no doubt he had killed before. The certainty of it resonated through him.

Obviously, some things amnesia couldn't erase.

"I can make arrangements—"

"No, Dad. No arrangements. If he isn't wanted for murder, he soon will be."

"He carries a gun, Grace. One that might be a murder weapon. Do realize the implications of that?"

"Do you mean to your reputation or to my safety?"

"For once in your life, don't be irresponsible," Charles retorted impatiently. "So far this morning, we've been fortunate. It won't take long for the police to show up on your doorstep. Then what will you do?" Charles's gaze dropped to her stomach. "It's not just you I'm concerned for. You're not thinking about—"

"We agreed last night that it's not your decision."

"I'm required by law to report a gunshot

wound," Charles snapped. "If I don't, I could lose my practice."

"Do what you have to do, Dad," she answered, the truth lying bitter against her tongue. It wasn't the first time she'd defied him. But a few moments earlier, when his eyes moved from her stomach back to her face, it was the first time she'd ever seen fear etched in his features.

"Damn it, Grace. I don't want to turn this into the same old argument. The man was shot. Your friend was killed. This is not about the fact that once again I'm choosing my practice over—"

"Over what? Me?" Grace rubbed the back of her neck, trying to loosen the tension. Even she couldn't ask him to go against his oath. "You're right, Dad." She sighed. "I put you in this position with my phone call and I'm sorry." The words were sad, made so by their unending conflict. "But I'm not going to budge on my decision, either. He stays with me until we figure this out."

Jacob had been about to agree with the doctor. No matter who he was, hiding behind a woman wasn't acceptable. But the undercurrent of emotion in the room changed his mind. Something wasn't being said and Jacob wanted to know what it was. Better to wait and get the information from the daughter.

"I'm safer with Jacob. Trust me, Dad." When he said nothing, she added, "Please."

Finally, it was Charles who turned away. "The pain is going to get worse. You're going to need morphine in a short while, Jacob. Enough to take the edge off. I can give you some but I have to go get the prescription filled." He closed his bag and turned to his daughter. "I'll be back in an hour."

The threat was there, Jacob knew. He had less than an hour to find out what the hell was going on.

Chapter Six

"Why didn't you tell him?"

"Tell him what?" Jacob asked.

"That you won't take the morphine he's bringing back."

She was right, of course. He couldn't risk being doped up if trouble started. "For a person who doesn't know me, you understand me pretty well," he commented dryly.

"One doesn't discount the other," she countered. Her gazed drifted over his face. "You've lost weight."

"Really?" Jacob's mouth twisted derisively. "I wouldn't know."

"Yes, well—"

"I didn't tell him I didn't want the morphine because I thought you needed some breathing room," he lied. "But I agree with your father, Grace."

"A man you just met."

"Technically, I've just met you, too."

Her body grew rigid. "You remembered Aspen."

He'd hurt her with his comment. A vulnerability he could take advantage of, if needed. "I stand corrected."

"For the record, I agree with my father, too." At Jacob's raised eyebrow, she added, "To a certain point. But that doesn't mean I can do what he wants. We need to get you out of here before he gets back."

"We?"

"I have to find out what happened last night and you're my only lead to the answers."

"I thought I was to have bed rest."

"I couldn't risk his overhearing anything else," she said impatiently. "He would've stopped us. You're not safe here."

"What if I don't ever remember, Grace?" When she didn't answer, he continued, "Why not let the police handle it?"

"They can't be trusted. Not yet. Not until we find out who killed Helene. Don't you see?"

"If I remember right, the police are the ones who find murderers."

Her head snapped up, and what he saw was genuine fear. "Not if they've already decided on a suspect."

"Me." When he tried to maneuver his feet to the floor, she placed a hand against his good shoulder.

"Please, let me help you. If you move too

fast, you could break open the stitching." Before he could stop them, her fingers drifted across his skin.

He caught her wrist, but this time with gentle fingers. His intent was to stop her, but the action brought her closer.

He caught her scent, breathed it in. Without thought, his thumb skimmed her pulse. When it jumped, his did, too. Slowly, he pulled her toward him until her hand rested against his chest. Her eyes met his and what he saw made him stop. The desire was there, but more than that, he saw panic.

He let her go. "I'm not so weak I can't put a pair of pants on."

Pink flushed her cheeks, but from embarrassment or temper, he wasn't sure.

She stepped back, letting her hands drop to her sides, but not before she made them into fists.

Temper, then.

When she walked to the closet, her actions were fluid, almost regal. And when she yanked open the door, he almost smiled.

She skimmed the hangers with her hand, pulled out a pair of slacks and a sweater. Judging from the high-end material of the charcoal V-neck sweater and the black chino slacks, he wasn't hurting for money.

"These should do."

"I guess they will." When he reached to take the hangers from her, pain exploded in his shoulder. He swore and grabbed at his arm, locking it to his side. "I'm going to need your car."

She tossed the clothes onto the corner of the bed. "Don't be stupid. You're not in any condition to drive."

He had to give the woman credit; she did snooty with a certain sex appeal.

"You're going to need someone to get you around."

Pointedly, he glanced at his gun. "I have a feeling I'm pretty self-sufficient."

But what he wasn't was flush. He needed cash.

Money, he knew, would open many more doors. "Did I have a wallet?"

She picked a slim, brown wallet from the dresser and handed it to him. "There's almost a thousand dollars, a few credit cards and your driver's license in there."

Instead of opening the billfold, Jacob laid it on the bed beside him. He'd search through it after she left the room.

"Now, do you want my help dressing?"

"No, I can handle it myself." He was in no mood to deal with the fluttery touch of her hands against him again.

"There's a brand-new toothbrush in the

bathroom's medicine cabinet and fresh towels on the rack," she noted, then walked over and turned on the bathroom light for him. "You're not strong enough yet to take a shower. And even if you think you are, you can't risk getting your bandages wet."

"I'll manage." He leaned back against the headboard and studied her through half-closed eyes.

"You didn't take me to the hospital because I'd be vulnerable." The fear was back with his statement, tightening her features, only for a heartbeat but long enough for him to see. And understand.

"Running will only protect me for so long. And like your father said, puts you at risk whether you're with me or not."

"I told you I want answers. And once your memory returns I'll get them," she replied. "And I'm hoping neither of us will need protection."

"About my other scars." When her eyebrow lifted in question, he clarified. "You wouldn't know how I acquired them, would you?"

"No. We were never that close," she replied evenly. But at what cost, he thought.

"Then why is it that little bits I am remembering seem to revolve around you?" Even without her reaction to him a few minutes prior, his instincts were telling him they'd been intimate. The tightening of his groin, the itch at the base of his spine, told him that if he didn't watch himself, they just might be again.

"Maybe because I knew Helene."

"Maybe," he replied, but he didn't believe it. "Do you have a picture of her?"

"Yes." She went to her dresser and slid open the top drawer. After a moment of digging, she pulled out a newspaper photo. She crossed the room and gave it to Jacob. "This was taken the day we opened The Tens. Our bar. Her bar," she corrected, then sighed. "Actually, I have no idea whose bar it is now."

"We need to find out," he decided. "Could be the new owner wanted a premature switching of titles and I got in the way." He studied the picture. It was a waist-to-head shot. Even with that, Jacob could tell the woman was tall and on the athletic side but not enough to detract from her overall femininity. He glanced at the deep cut of the buttoned jacket with no blouse to ruin the sleek, cool effect of the navy business suit.

One of Helene's arms was casually looped around Grace's shoulders. Her hair was a deep red, spiked softly around the sharp angles of her cheeks, emphasizing a long nose, its feminine point.

"Do you recognize her?"

"No," he said, taking one last look before glancing up. "Can I keep this?"

When she nodded, he placed it by his wallet. "Do you need help to the bathroom?"

He contemplated the wide span of hardwood floor between him and the bathroom door. "I can manage," he said and hoped he was right.

"Then I'll make you some toast. And some coffee." She turned to leave.

He waited until she reached the door. "Grace. Were you telling the truth earlier? Are you absolutely sure I didn't kill Helene?"

She hesitated for a moment, her hand clenched on the doorknob. "I'm not absolutely sure of anything. Least of all, you."

JACOB COULDN'T SAY he felt better, but he felt more human after cleaning up and putting on clean clothes. The itch was off his skin and his stomach had settled. His shoulder and head still throbbed, but he managed to find some aspirin in her cabinet. He'd found a razor and new blades also, but decided against a shave. No use causing more damage with a shaky hand.

Like the bedroom, the bath had a decidedly feminine appeal. The combination hardwood floor and bead-board paneling presented a casual coziness that was only emphasized by a pedestal sink, distressed vanity and an eclectic collection of candles.

Curious, Jacob grabbed the shampoo from the corner of the bathtub. He took a whiff, then read the bottle. Honeysuckle.

A small mystery solved.

For the first time, he simply focused on the facts of his situation and systematically sorted through what he'd learned over the last half hour.

In his mind, he saw flashes of pictures. From parks to fields to coliseums. He couldn't bring names to mind, or locations. He couldn't say if he'd been to these locations or merely seen them in photos or on television. They held no connection to him on any level.

The only thing, only person who seemed familiar to him was Grace.

A lead—his only instinctive lead. One he planned on pursuing.

The coffee aroma hit him as he stepped out of the bedroom. "Smells good."

The neutral colors, the rustic pine floors triggered no memories, but this time he hadn't expected them to. "How often have I been here?"

"Many times. Too many to count."

The walk to the kitchen caused his legs to shake. Enough that he was grateful for the stool when he slid onto it.

"Go ahead and have some while I get things together." She placed a travel mug in front of him, along with a plate with toast. "You liked your coffee black."

He lifted the mug. "Let's see if I still do." When he took a swig, the heat of it punched him in the belly. Enough to make him grunt and draw a slanted look from Grace. "It's good. Thanks."

"You're welcome." She grabbed two chocolate chip cookies from a nearby plate.

"So, do you and your father disagree often?"

"No more often than most fathers and daughters." She came around the counter and leaned a hip against the side. "I turned on the news while you were getting dressed and checked my computer. The shooting wasn't mentioned on either."

"You just changed the subject."

"You noticed." She took a bite of her cookie, chewed, then waved the remaining piece like a pointer. "Helene's death should have made the morning news."

"A murder would be hard to keep out of the

press," he reasoned, even as a cookie crumb settled on her cheek, distracting him. "But the police have done it before."

Giving in to the urge, he leaned in and brushed the crumb away with the pad of his thumb. But instead of keeping the touch light, the gesture simple, he found himself cupping her face in his palm—told himself that he was only searching for memories. Answers.

"Jacob—"

"Shh." His thumb stopped her mouth, mid-motion, leaving her lips slightly parted. He slipped between to the warm smooth touch of her teeth, felt her intake of breath rush over his skin—

The doorbell sounded, jolting them both apart.

Jacob swore, low and mean. His body went rigid, his hand already reaching for the gun in his back waistband. "Your father?"

"He wouldn't ring the bell," she answered,

trying to get her heart back down from her throat. Not from the interruption but from the realization that in another minute, probably less if she were honest, she'd have been in Jacob's arms.

"Is your car out front?"

"Yes. It's parked under my carport."

"Then you'd better answer." Jacob's face turned cold, almost savage. The fact he reached for his gun only fed her trepidation.

"Leave my plate. It will look like you're eating breakfast alone. I'll wait in the bedroom," he whispered while he checked his clip. "But I'll be watching, so no worries." This time when he cupped her cheek, it was for reassurance. "You'll be okay. Just stay calm."

After Jacob disappeared into the bedroom, she walked slowly to the front door.

A second chime rang out just as she peered

through the peephole. Two men stood on her front porch, both dressed in navy-blue suits, both holding badges in their hand. The law enforcement insignias glared in the sunlight.

"Who is it?"

"Annapolis Police, Miss Renne. We need to speak with you."

Her hand tightened reflexively on the knob. She glanced at the closed bedroom, unlocked the dead bolt and opened the front door. "Can I help you?"

"Miss Renne?" At her nod, the thinner of the two, a nearly bald man with a flat face and heavy eyelids, stepped forward.

"I'm Detective Webber." He pointed to his partner, a man with steroid-typical muscles packed into a tailored suit and crisp, white shirt. "This is Detective Sweeney. We're both with the Annapolis Police. Homicide Division."

"How are you, Miss Renne?" Sweeney's

smile was a grim line but it was his gaze that drew her attention. Gray eyes studied her from under two rather thick eyebrows, before shifting past her shoulder to sweep the room behind her.

Grace resisted the urge to shut the door. "Fine, but uncertain how I can help you, Detective."

First one, then the other flipped his badge closed and pocketed it. "Can we talk to you about Helene Garrett?" Sweeney asked, his gaze back on hers.

"My bar manager called me earlier about her death and I'm really not up to answering any questions just now."

"You mean your ex-manager, don't you?" Sweeney placed his foot in the doorway. "It's either here or downtown, Miss Renne. Your choice," he advised. His tone, while professional, left her with no alternative but to believe him. "We have a murderer on the loose. What happened to your friend wasn't a robbery or an accident. And I'm sure you would want her killer caught as soon as possible."

"Of course, I do."

"The longer we wait, the less chance we have of catching him." Sweeney pushed against the door with his knee with just enough pressure to emphasize his point—if she wanted them to get physical, they would.

"All right, gentlemen." Grace released the door, allowing the two men to enter. She led them to the middle of the room, but didn't offer them a seat. "How can I help you?"

"You can start by telling us where you were last night at approximately eleven o'clock." Webber fished under his suit and pulled out a notebook and pen.

"I was here baking cookies." She gestured to the plate on the counter.

Neither man glanced over. "Was anyone here with you?" Webber continued.

"I'm afraid not."

"Did Helene Garrett have any enemies? Anyone who might have wanted her dead?" Sweeney asked. Once again those gray eyes skimmed the room, touching on the closed bedroom door before moving over to the window and back to Grace.

Grace shifted until she blocked his line of sight. "No one that I know of."

"How about her friends?" Webber remarked, his frustration breaking through. "Do you know anyone who was close enough to Miss Garrett to give some insight into the last few days of her life?"

"Helene didn't have friends, she had business acquaintances. Too many for me to know."

"You mean to tell us that after three years of being partners, you have no idea how Helene

Garrett conducted her life? Who she associated with? Can't make a guess at who could have killed her?"

Grace hesitated.

Are you absolutely sure I didn't kill Helene?
No.

She put her hands in her sweatshirt pouch and pressed her palms against her stomach. She felt the weight of her baby against the burden of her decision.

The police would do their best to keep her safe. But she understood deep down that their best would not be good enough.

"I'm telling you exactly that, Detective Webber," she said. "Helene was a private person. She didn't share much about herself with anyone. And I wasn't her only partner. Her capital was tied into many business ventures."

"We're finding that out," Sweeney admitted

wryly. "You recently sold your half of the club to her, right?"

"That's right."

"Did you know the new owner is Jacob Lomax? He was one of those business acquaintances you mentioned earlier." The shock of Sweeney's statement nearly shattered her rigid hold. But then Webber smiled with venom and Grace's nervousness gave way to anger.

"No, I didn't know Mr. Lomax was the new owner, but I'm not surprised."

"How well did you know him?"

"Not very well at all. In fact, I didn't remember him until you just mentioned his name. I met him briefly, about eight months ago, but shared no more than a handshake." Grace and Jacob had kept their affair private. But if the police dug deep enough, they would discover the truth.

"Even if I had known, it wouldn't have mattered." She nodded at the boxes in the living room. "As you can see, I'm moving. Out of state, actually. And I didn't want to manage a business long-distance. Helene understood that."

"Can I ask why you are moving?" Sweeney walked over to the nearest box and lifted the flap.

Grace swallowed a nasty comment about minding his own business. "A change of climate."

"When was last time you saw her?" Sweeney asked, before returning. He glanced over to the counter, took in the breakfast dishes.

Another lie was there on the tip of her tongue. But too many people could have known about their meeting the day before. "Yesterday at the bistro down on Main. We had lunch together. A farewell of sorts."

"Do you mind?" He nodded toward the cookies.

"Not at all."

"Thanks." Sweeney helped himself to a cookie, took a bite and nodded his approval. "You and Miss Garrett parted on good terms?"

"Yes, we did." The hair prickled at her nape. There was no doubt in her mind that Jacob was observing her conversation with the detectives. "Is that all, gentlemen?"

"For now." Sweeney finished his cookie in one more bite, then reached into his suit pocket and pulled out a business card. "If you think of anything else that might help us, please contact me."

Grace didn't take the card from him fast enough and it dropped between them. Sweeney bent down to retrieve it and paused, his eyes on the hardwood floor. "Miss Renne, did I mention that Helene

Garrett managed to shoot her killer just before she died?"

"No, Detective. You didn't. But I don't see how that—"

"There are bloodstains on your floor."

Grace followed his line of vision. More than a few red streaks smeared the varnished cherrywood. Marks she'd missed in her hasty cleanup the night before. "Those are mine. I cut my foot yesterday on some broken glass. I must have missed a few spots when I cleaned up."

Sweeney automatically looked at her bare feet. "There's no bandage."

"It was a small cut." Her chin lifted. "I'm not going to show you the bottom of my feet, Detective."

"She's lying," Webber inserted, obviously pleased by the prospect. He shoved his notebook back into his pocket.

Indignation worked its way into her words.

"You honestly cannot think that I'm somehow involved in Helene's death—"

"You're right, I don't." Sweeney stood, scuffed the stains with his foot. "Where is he?"

Webber took a threatening step toward Grace. Out of sheer willpower, she stood her ground.

"Where is who?"

The blow came from out of nowhere. Pain ripped through her cheek, burst behind her eyes. She staggered back, just managing to keep herself from hitting the floor.

"My partner is much more polite than I am," Webber warned. "Where is Jacob Lomax?"

Grace straightened, her legs shaking. She could taste blood on her lip, but her hand automatically went to her belly. "I told you I haven't seen the man in months."

When Webber raised his fist again, a gun exploded from behind Grace. Screaming, the big man doubled over, one meaty hand wrapped around the other. Blood oozed through his fingers and dripped to the floor.

"Move, Grace." The words came low and mean. Grace automatically stepped out of reach, giving Jacob an unobstructed view of the two men.

"Looking for me?" With one shoulder against the doorsill, Jacob shifted his 9 mm slightly until it pointed at Sweeney. Jacob's face hardened into savage lines.

Slowly, Sweeney raised his arms away from his sides, but shock flickered across his face before he masked it. "I am if you're Lomax."

"That's what I hear."

"You son of a bitch," Webber wheezed. He slumped to his knees and cradled his injured hand to his chest. "You just shot a police officer."

Jacob let out a derisive snort, ignoring Webber's gasps of pain. "Most cops don't hit potential female witnesses. Or wear suits that cost more than a year's salary."

Sweat broke out on Jacob's forehead. Grace could see the tremors in his left hand and understood he wouldn't stay standing very long.

He tilted his gun, just a bit to put Sweeney's chest in his crosshairs. "Want to try telling me who you both really are?"

"We work for a private investor that is extremely interested in your relationship with Helene Garrett," Sweeney answered, cautious.

"And this is how you get your information?" Jacob mocked. Out of his peripheral vision, he caught Grace wiping the blood from her lip. Rage strained against reason, pushing the limit of his control. "I think you boys need to work on your approach."

With a growl, Webber grabbed for his gun. Jacob fired and Webber stumbled back. Blood flooded from the man's neck. He struggled, groping the wound with his hands even as he crumpled choking on his own blood.

Sweeney charged Grace. Reacting swiftly, she slid on her hip, taking out his legs and toppled Sweeney like a bowling pin.

Jacob slammed his pistol into Sweeney's head, knocking him out cold. "Let's see how you like headaches," he murmured, then dropped to his knees, shaking.

"Jacob!" Grace sat beside him. Immediately, she found herself drawn tight against his side. "I thought—"

"Are you all right?"

"Yes." Grace leaned into him, grasped his sweater in one hand to make sure he didn't pull away. Finding reassurance. Just for a moment, she buried her face against his chest. He smelled of soap. Basic. Clean. Reassuring against the heavy metallic scent of blood that already thickened the air.

"Do you need help?" she asked.

"Not yet." He blew air out through his mouth, trying to get a grip on his rolling stomach, his shaking limbs. "Who in the hell taught you how to take someone down like that?"

"You did." She tried to smile, but her lips wobbled. "That day in the snow."

Chapter Seven

"Looks like you were right." Jacob found handcuffs on Webber's belt and snapped them on Sweeney's wrists. "Do you have any cash?"

"About a hundred dollars."

"Make sure you grab it," he ordered. "And your keys."

The scent of blood grew to a sickening stench. Grace glanced down at Webber, his face now a contorted death mask of crimson. His expensive suit was no more than a soggy towel saturated with his blood.

With effort, she took a few deep breaths through her mouth to avoid the scent, drive away the nausea.

"Are you going to faint on me?"

"No." She dug her nails into her palm to prove it.

Swearing, he grabbed a throw from the couch and covered Webber's body. "That's the best I can do for you, Grace."

"Thank you." Her voice quivered, but with Webber covered, the queasiness started to fade. "Aren't we going to question Sweeney?"

"Questioning a prisoner takes stamina. I don't have any right now." He checked the two men's pockets, pulled out their wallets. "Let's see if they are who they said they were." He took out the badges. "Fake. Crafted well, though."

"How do you know?" Her panic faded under curiosity.

"Just do." Jacob shrugged, storing the information away for later. He was working on instinct and right now it was telling him to move. "But like my weapons training, I couldn't tell you how long I've had the knowledge or where I picked it up from."

He took the money from each of the wallets. "Whoever pays them pays them well. They're carrying over three thousand between the two of them." He handed her the cash. "We're going to need this. Credit cards put us out on the information grid."

"You were carrying almost as much in your wallet."

"Maybe we have the same boss," he answered derisively.

"Sweeney was in charge. If that's his real name. Anyone with this caliber of forgeries, probably works under a dozen different aliases." He patted a few more pockets until he found their keys and cell phones. He glanced at the phones. "All the numbers are deleted. These boys knew what they were doing. Still, if his boss decides to call, I want to be available." He pocketed Sweeney's cell phone, then handed Webber's phone to her.

"Crush it." Jacob's face paled to a sickly gray; his lips were bloodless. A sheen of perspiration covered his skin, dampened his hair. "I'd like to know what the hell they want from me."

Grace stomped on the phone, shattering it. If he was placing his life on the line, the least he deserved was the truth. "It's not you they want, Jacob."

"Say that again."

"It's not you," she repeated, grinding the last of the phone under her heel. "It's me."

He sat back. "Go on. I'm listening."

"Last night, you were still conscious when

I found you. In fact, you knocked on the door, then collapsed on the porch."

She rubbed the back of her neck, suddenly feeling the weight of the world there. "You told me to hide. That someone wanted to kill me."

"I didn't say who."

"No. You didn't."

"Grace, Sweeney came looking for me. Not you."

Startled, she could only look at him. "You're right. He wasn't concerned with me at all. But that doesn't make sense."

"It does if we're dealing with two separate problems," he reasoned.

"You mean we're being chased by two different people?" She dropped to her knees, her hands braced on her legs. Her gaze was fixed on his. "But it still doesn't answer why whoever wants me came after you and Helene first. I can be found by anyone who has a phone book."

"Maybe someone chased me to your house and I was afraid you would get in the way," he reasoned. "Or maybe I was just delirious from my head injury."

"No, the threat was real," Grace argued. "I'm sure of it."

"And since I brought the message, you think you can trust me to help you?"

She looked pointedly at his shoulder. "That's what friends do," she whispered. "Besides, who else can I trust if it isn't the guy who warned me?"

After a moment, he nodded. "Okay, pal, grab whatever you can hold in your pockets. We don't have time for anything else." Jacob tossed Sweeney's keys under her couch. He was standing by the time she returned from the bedroom. "What kind of car do you drive?"

"A Jag," she shouted from the bedroom. "I filled the tank yesterday."

"Good. We might need something with some power."

She pushed her wallet into her sweatshirt pocket and phone into the back of her jeans. She grabbed her keys off the counter.

Before she could react, he opened the front door and fired a few bullets into Sweeney's tires. "How well can you drive?"

She glanced at the deflated tires and thought of Webber. "Better than you can shoot."

THE JAG WAS THE COLOR of hot salsa, with saber-chromed wheels and butter-cream leather seats. If a car could preen, this one would have a reason.

"Nice ride." Drained, Jacob shifted back into the passenger seat. The throb in his shoulder took on an edge of heat. He shifted using the armrest to brace his bad shoulder. What he needed was some time to regain strength and to sort through their situation.

"Thanks. That's what you said when you helped me pick it out."

"I did?"

"I wasn't lying to you," she replied. "We were friends." But like *father,* he noted, she infused no warmth into the word *friend.*

"Were we more than friends?" It seemed natural to cock his head, lift one eyebrow.

"No," she said, but with enough hesitation to feed his doubt.

"Am I gay?"

Her lips curled into a tolerant smile. "No."

"Are you?"

She laughed then. "No."

He decided he liked her laugh. It rolled through her, erupting in a slightly breathless chuckle. He realized he wanted to hear it again.

Her gaze turned to the road and he used the opportunity to take a long look. He took in the slope of her neck, the pulse at the base of her throat. A flush crept up over her cheeks, telling him she was aware of his scrutiny, but Jacob continued to study her nonetheless.

He'd distanced himself from his emotions, accepting the situation. Though, even at its best, it was nothing more than a maze of smoke and mirrors.

But something inside—an echo of what was, or what could've been—kept him from gaining that same emotional distance from her.

"You're sure we weren't more to each other?"

"Yes," she said, exasperated. The pulse quickened, the flush darkened. Her response was more than a little breathless, but this time there was no chuckle.

Did her reaction mean they had been

involved and she was lying, or she'd thought about it and was embarrassed? Self-preservation either way, Jacob decided. And that he could understand.

"What happened?" This time the push wasn't for the truth, but for the reaction. Damn, he found her blush charming.

"Nothing really. You left."

He rested his head against the window, enjoyed the cool glass against the pounding in his temple. "What do you mean? Did I leave the state? Or leave the country?"

"Both." *You left me,* Grace thought, keeping her pride intact but at the cost of another crack in her heart.

"So why did I leave?"

"I don't know." At least in that Grace could be truthful. She downshifted, taking a hairpin turn with the ease of a race car driver. She heard his reluctant grunt of approval. "You never explained. One day you were here, the next you weren't."

"Can't say I was a very good friend, then."

"You had no reason to be, really." She stopped the ache that threatened to harden the edges of her response. Just.

"How long had we known each other?"

"Not long," Grace hesitated, pretending to do the calculations. "Two months. Almost three." Eighty-one days.

Jacob realized she was choosing her words very carefully. A person only did that when they didn't want to offend or, more importantly, wanted to defend. From the white-knuckled grip she had on the steering wheel, he tended to believe her choice was the latter.

"I had accidentally interrupted a business meeting between you and Helene. I didn't know you were in our office and I burst through the door all excited about a jazz band

I had just booked. One we'd been trying to get for months. She introduced us."

Helene again. Shooting Sweeney's partner had showed Jacob he was capable of killing. He'd felt no remorse, not even a twinge of regret. Webber needed killing. Period. But somehow Helene's murder didn't sit right. Almost as if murdering her didn't fit his sense of self.

"What you told Sweeney about Helene, was it true?"

"More or less," she acknowledged. "We had lunch together and she gave me the final copies of our sales contract. We ate. We laughed. We hugged. We cried a little, then said goodbye."

"What did you talk about?"

"Business details. Plans to meet again," Grace said, then glanced in his direction. "You."

"What about me?"

"She told me she was meeting you later that night and wanted to know if I had a message to pass on." Actually, Helene had threatened to tell Jacob about the baby. "I said no."

"I see." Grace's fingers flexed against the steering wheel. "Did anyone stop by your table?"

"Only the waiter," she said. "But he's been there forever."

"How about her demeanor? Did she seem angry? Afraid?"

"No—" She stopped. "Wait. When I came back from the bathroom after we ate, she seemed…" Grace thought for a moment. "Impatient."

"She could've been spooked."

"Or she could've had a hard time saying goodbye."

"Maybe. But if she kept herself distant, why would she be upset?"

"At least she said goodbye." The retort was out of her mouth before she could stop it. "I'm sorry, that was unfair."

"Why? Because I don't remember?"

Her lips smoothed out into a grin. "Well, it does put you at a disadvantage, doesn't it?"

"I suppose it does." Then seriously, he added, "I'd like to think I had a good reason, Grace. Maybe it even has something to do with what we're in now. But either way, if and when I do remember, I'll tell you everything."

Grace shook her head. "I don't expect you to—"

"I know," he said quietly. "Why would Helene leave me the bar?"

"She trusted you."

"But why didn't she leave it to you?"

"I told her I wasn't coming back to Maryland."

"Did Helene give you anything? Warn you about anything?"

"Nothing," she answered. "I told you, it was like every other lunch we've had together. Other than saying goodbye, of course."

"Did Helene ever talk about me? I mean, before the lunch?"

"No. Never. Her business was her business."

"Yet you trusted her."

"Implicitly," Grace said without hesitation.

"Why?"

"I don't know. Instinct, I guess."

"Is that why we became friends? Because you instinctively like me?"

"You could be charming when you wanted to be." Again there was no hesitation.

He watched the roadside for a moment. A few mailboxes, some scattered buildings. Remote, but not so remote a person had to travel far for food or fuel. "It's frustrating. I know this road, yet I'd swear to you that I've never seen it before."

Grace laid her hand on his thigh and squeezed. "It will come. We need to give it time."

"That's the problem, if Sweeney is any indication. We don't have time."

"So I'll tell you what I can and hope it prods your memories."

"That bothers me, too," he acknowledged. "After three months of being together, the only information I shared with you was my name? And that I'm a business associate of your ex-partner?"

"Yes." Sadness underlined her words, not resentment. "That's why I left, isn't it?" His eyes flitted over her, the blue in them flat and unreadable. "Because you pushed me to open up?"

"I told you I don't know why you left." More buildings loomed as they passed a sign welcoming them to Eastport. She glanced at the side mirror and changed lanes. "You didn't share that with me, either."

"Talk about irony." His laugh was harsh,

tinged with self-deprecation. "If I had told you about myself, we both might have a better idea about the mess we're in. Even my driver's license is from out of state."

"Jacob, Helene had moved out of her place and into yours a few months ago. She told me she'd rather rent from a friend than a stranger. But she didn't advertise it. She told me she needed some peace and quiet away from work."

"Where?"

"You have a renovated boathouse. Down south off of the bay."

"And you were going to tell me this when?"

"Excuse me for being distracted," she muttered.

"Point taken." His sigh was long, ragged. "I guess that's where we're headed, then. If Helene left any clues behind, it would be either there or at the club."

"Shouldn't we go by the club first?

Jacob shook his head. "The police will be watching it. I'm not up for another confrontation."

"You might have spoken too soon." Grace glanced at her rearview mirror. "I think we're being followed."

Jacob studied the side mirror. "The black sedan?"

"Yes."

"Turn your blinker on like you're going to turn right. Then take the next left."

Grace gripped the steering wheel, taking the turn on a squeal of tires.

A few moments later, the black sedan skidded around the corner. The driver gunned its engine, picking up pursuit.

"Looks like I didn't smack our friend hard enough," Jacob commented dryly. He pulled out his gun and checked the clip.

Grace punched the gas.

"How did he get a car so fast?" Grace demanded.

"Why don't you ask the guy in the passenger seat with the machine gun?"

Grace didn't take her eyes off the street. Instead, she swung the Jag into a sharp right. The back end fishtailed, but a second later Grace regained control.

The traffic light flashed red at the end of the block. "Run it," Jacob ordered.

"Hold on." Grace dodged a delivery truck with another twist of the wheel but didn't ease up on the accelerator. Pedestrians scattered, screaming as they dove for the curb.

Rubber squealed against cement. Bullets pinged off her side panel. "Are they crazy?"

"You don't have to be crazy to kill." His fist hit the window button before he released the safety belt and swung around in his seat. He thrust the gun out the window and fired at Sweeney.

"There's too many people, Jacob." Real fear caught hold of her. One slip, one bad reaction, and she could kill an innocent person.

A taxi cab skidded across the intersection. Grace slammed the brakes and wrenched the wheel, spinning the car into a one-eighty. People screamed and scattered, diving and ducking behind parked cars.

Jacob's shoulder slammed against the passenger door. Pain ripped through him from his elbow to his skull.

Swearing, Jacob righted himself and fired a few more shots. "Keep the car straight, damn it."

"You're kidding, right?" She shoved the stick into Reverse and hit the accelerator. Jacob's back crashed into the dash. Metal crunched metal as she hit the car behind her. She threw the Jag into gear, heard the whine of steel breaking loose from the back end.

"Was that straight enough for you? I just lost my bumper." Not waiting for a reply, Grace charged through the pattern of cars clogging the city streets, weaving when she could, cutting others off when she had to.

Grace hit her brakes, barely missing the back end of a bus.

Suddenly, their friends in the sedan skidded past them. Sweeney slammed the brakes, fishtailing against a corner mailbox.

Jacob's bullets pelted the sedan, doing very little damage to their windows. "The glass is bulletproof."

Sweeney reversed on a squeal of tires. Wide black stripes burned the pavement, smoked the air.

Grace floored the accelerator and shot forward, once again putting them into a two-vehicle race.

"Construction?" She nearly screamed the

word. Orange barrels spotted the street in uneven lines, narrowing into a blockade across the highway on-ramp.

"We need that ramp, Grace. We can lose them on the stretch without traffic lights."

"You're out of your mind, Lomax." The back window exploded, shooting shards of glass into the air.

"Scoot down, damn it."

Grace couldn't get down far, not if she wanted to keep control of the car.

Jacob dropped his empty clip and shoved the second into his pistol. "They're using the machine guns. I can't hold them off very much longer."

"Damn!" She hit the steering wheel with one fist.

"Take the ramp." Jacob punctuated the statement with two shots from his gun through the back opening.

The sedan sped up, closing the distance between him and Grace's car. Close enough that Grace could see Sweeney in the driver's seat.

Grace waited a long few seconds, swerved toward the blockade of wood and barrels, her foot heavy against the accelerator.

The Jag hit the barrier, jolting them both. She gritted her teeth. "This car isn't even a year old."

"At the rate we're going, we'll probably be dead before the day's over. So I'm not too worried about it."

She pushed away thoughts of her baby. "Not if I can help it."

In the distance, she heard sirens. Felt the prickle at her back. "Hold on." Grace took the car flying over the dirt and broken cement.

Police cars raced toward them, their red and blue lights flashing, their sirens screeching.

"We need to lose your car. It's too conspicuous."

"You think?" Grace commented as two more police cars joined the chase.

"You've got five cop cars on your ass."

"I saw. Now all we need is a chopper and we can have a party." Grace swerved, just missing a parked construction backhoe. One of the police cars wasn't so lucky. It bounced off the digger, spun and hit another cop car head-on. Air bags exploded. Grace said a small prayer hoping the bags did their job.

"Two down," Jacob said, his voice grim.

Wheels hit flat cement and Grace shoved the car into high gear. The Jag raced onto the expressway.

"Let's see what we can do with some elbow room." When she floored the accelerator this time, Jacob saw the needle shoot past one hundred.

Grace jerked the wheel sending the car onto the shoulder, creating her own lane as she passed cars one by one.

"Don't tell me. I taught you this on the mountain, too."

"No, we only had time for some light hand-to-hand combat," she said, and swerved two lanes to the right without touching the brake. "I learned this on my own."

The sirens behind them lessened, telling Grace the police cars were losing ground.

"Where are our friends?"

Jacob dropped his clip, checked the number of rounds left, shoved it back in. "Lost them when the police joined the party."

He glanced up and caught the sign for Chesapeake Bay. "Take this street."

"It leads to the harbor. Limits our options."

"Take it."

She saw the blood-soaked shirt, the gray-tinged skin. He'd ripped open his stitches and was losing blood. "Are you okay?"

"I'll manage."

The pier loomed ahead. Monday midmorning traffic had already congested the main path with tourists.

A barrage of bullets hit the car from the side. Suddenly, Sweeney was there again. This time close enough for Grace to see the grim slant of his features. "Where did he come from?"

"Look out!"

Grace swerved, barely missing a biker and his dog. But it cost them. The car slammed through the metal guard gate blocking the pedestrian's crossing and shot down the main pier. People screamed and scattered in mass panic. Grace slammed on the brakes, but there wasn't enough time.

The car skidded, the tires screeched. A

heartbeat later, the car splintered the side railing and plunged into the water.

More screams shattered the air.

But this time, Grace realized, they were hers.

Chapter Eight

When the car hit the water, both air bags exploded, driving Grace back into her seat. Instinctively she struggled against the bags' suffocating weight. Water rushed in from the floor, a gush of icy liquid that sucked the oxygen out of the car, smothering what little gasps of air she managed.

Without warning, the car shifted nose up. Water gushed through the blown-out back window. Tossed backward, Grace stifled a scream. She clawed at the bag, trying to get leverage.

"Stop struggling, Grace." The order came in a short burst of air by her ear. Suddenly her safety belt broke free. "Hold your breath!"

The car submerged. Her breath backed up into her lungs. Out of nowhere, Jacob grabbed her hand and tugged her toward him. Blindly, she shoved the deflating air bag away.

Jacob pulled her through the back window behind him. The ragged steel scraped at her sweatshirt, snagging her like a fish on a line. Panic pressed in on her chest. She yanked on the material but it held tight. Quickly, she unzipped it and pulled free, leaving the jacket behind.

Her head broke the surface a few seconds before his. She dragged oxygen into her lungs in huge swallowing gulps. The gritty water and air burned her throat and lungs.

The black sedan skidded to a stop by a small diving equipment rental shack. Both men jumped from the car, but Sweeney's passenger was faster. A machine gun appeared in his hands a split second later.

"Dive!" Jacob ordered. Gunshots peppered the water in front of them.

She gasped for breath and plunged below again. This time swimming deep as bullets whizzed past her.

Only when the blood pounded at her ears and the air slipped from her lungs did she kick to the surface.

Jacob reached for the semiautomatic in his waistband just as Sweeney grabbed the machine gun and smashed it into the other man's face.

Jacob heard Grace surface, coughing. "Stay behind me." With his feet he tread water, ignoring the pain that seared his back and shoulders. Instead, he scanned the rental shack. Racks of oxygen tanks lined one side of the front door. Pedestrians scattered, running away from the gunmen.

Jacob didn't hesitate. He fired into the rack of divers' oxygen tanks. An explosion ripped through the air. The gunmen hit the deck, but Sweeney's partner was too close. A fire stream shot from the ground behind him, the flames engulfed the man.

Jacob looked at Grace. "Are you okay?"

When she nodded, he said, "Follow me."

Jacob swam under the nearby fishing piers, looped out and followed an invisible line of water down south. Several minutes later, both he and Grace rode the waves onto the beach well away from the crowd of onlookers at the pier fire.

"This isn't good, Jacob." Grace stood and let the water lap against her calves. Sand sucked at her feet. Her legs trembled, but with the effort from wading ashore or from sheer shock, she couldn't be sure.

"It's not done, either." He came abreast of her and stopped.

He was right, of course. She tried not to think about it. Instead, she pressed her hand to her belly, took comfort in the round swell of it, and then said a silent prayer that at least for now, they were all safe. "What's our next step?"

When Jacob didn't answer, Grace turned fully toward him. But his eyes weren't on her face.

Panic tripped down her spine as she followed his gaze to her stomach.

A thin cotton tank top stuck to her body, a second skin that outlined the fullness of her breasts, the more than slight roundness of her stomach. Her hand plucked at the material, pulling it away from the damp skin beneath.

But he barely noticed. His mind flashed back to Grace's house and her confrontation with Sweeney. He saw her hand dip to her belly when Webber hit her, saw her father's eyes drop to Grace's stomach during their argument.

"You're pregnant?" Suddenly, Jacob exploded with a string of curses.

"It seems you remembered some of your favorite words."

"You think this is a joke?" Pain ripped through his shoulder, down his arm. Bits of sand caught under his bandage, burned like acid in his wound. Sheer willpower kept him on his feet, fighting the waves that slammed against the back of his legs. "Since this morning, you've been shot at, punched and nearly drowned." He jabbed at the sky with his finger. "And the day isn't even half over yet." It wasn't a question, so he didn't expect an answer. But what he didn't expect was her chin to hitch, her eyes to narrow.

Her temper enraged his own. He grasped on to the anger with both hands, knowing if he didn't the thought of what could've happened—what might still happen—would make him shudder with fear. "How far along are you?"

"Almost five months."

He stood there for a moment, where the bay hugged the sandy shore, knowing that with her statement she'd just upped the risk. "Of all the idiotic—" He glanced at her, then stopped. Not because he'd gone too far. He was justified, damn it. But for the first time, he looked beyond her temper, beyond the stubbornness that kept her back rigid, her features tight. And he saw the hunted glaze of her eyes, the paleness of her skin.

The need to protect her rolled through him, knocking the breath from his chest. "Let's go." Annoyed, he shoved the pistol into his back waistband with his good hand and yanked his sweater over the handle. "Act normal."

Pregnant.

With a quick glance, he scanned their surroundings. The beach was fairly large with a parking lot that ran for more than a block. Just beyond lay a playground spotted with children and their parents.

"Stay down. Use the cars for cover."

Grace couldn't stop shivering. The brisk wind beat against her damp skin and jeans. "We're wet and you're bleeding." She nodded toward his shoulder. The sweater was more crimson than not across the shoulder and chest. "How normal do you think we can act?"

They walked briskly, cutting through several rows of cars, avoiding mingling families and other groups of people.

"Over here."

Farther down toward the back of the parking lot sat a truck with a camper shell attached to the bed. A classic, if you counted the early seventies, with more rust than paint across its hood and tailgate.

The driver's window stood half-open. Far enough for Jacob to reach in and unlock the door.

"Watch for trouble." Jacob opened the door, shoved over a baseball cap that lay on the seat. Shifting, he managed to squirm under the dashboard. He grabbed the wires from under the steering column and pulled them free.

"You're hot-wiring a car?" Grace scanned the surrounding area. She strained her ears for any signs of sirens but heard nothing but the wind whip through the cabin.

"It's better than walking." The engine revved, punctuating his remark. "Get in. You're driving."

Jacob maneuvered out from under the dash

and let out a long hiss when his shoulder bumped the steering wheel.

She needed no other prodding and slid into the driver's seat. "Let's go," Jacob ordered. Then he grabbed the baseball cap and shoved it onto her head. "Can you drive?"

"It's an automatic," she said, throwing the car into gear. "If I run into trouble, I'll make sure you're the first to know."

"You do that." Gas fumes and stale vinyl filled the air. Her stomach rolled in protest but Grace resisted the urge to hold her breath.

Within seconds, she backed them out of the parking spot and drove away. "Are we safe?"

"For the time being." He noticed her shivering. He reached over and switched on the heat. "Where's my house?"

"If we go there, they might be there waiting."

"Doesn't matter. It's a chance we're going

to have to take. Right now, that house might be the key to getting my memory back."

Grace tensed. Her home. Her father. "Jacob, I forgot about my dad." She groped at her pocket. "I need to warn him."

"Do you think you'll be doing him a favor?"

"What if he'd walked in on Sweeney?" She took her phone out of her pocket, biting back a curse when she flipped open the lid. The LED screen was cracked.

"Sweeney followed us too quickly." His eyes studied her for a moment. "Chances are that your father discovered Webber's body after Sweeney left. Which means he called the police. Which means he'll be questioned by the authorities—if he isn't being questioned already. He has no idea what happened. He can be honest with the police and tell them about me. Your father has no reason to trust me now. If you contact him, they'll know and realize you're not being kidnapped but a willing accomplice. We don't know who we're dealing and until we do, I'm not going to take a chance; it might be the police themselves."

"An informant?" She shook the water from the phone. When that didn't work, she used her teeth and popped open the back cover. Maybe if she dried off the battery and placed the phone to the heater vent…

"Let me do that."

"Not a chance. You'll throw it out the window." She glanced over at him. "My dad's better scared than dead? Is that what you're saying?" She balanced the phone across the steering wheel and used her finger nails to pry out the battery. "You think that my dad is involved with this?"

"Someone is holding Sweeney's leash. And until I discover who it is, the only person I'm sure didn't kill Helene is you."

"The only thing my father knows is that you are a friend of mine in trouble—"

The battery popped out and fell into her lap. Grace froze. "Jacob, there's a note."

"What?"

"A small note folded in half." She took out the thin strip of wet paper that clung to the underside of the battery and handed it to him.

Carefully he separated the back from the front. "It's a series of letters and numbers." Quickly, he counted them.

Grace shot him a side glance. "It's Helene's handwriting," she said. "Are they readable?"

"Yes. Only the edges are smeared a little," Jacob replied. "Did Helene have access to your phone yesterday?"

Did she? Grace went over the lunch yesterday in her mind. "I turned my phone off because I didn't want to be interrupted during lunch. We were sitting in a booth, so I set my keys and phone on the window ledge."

"Why not in your purse?"

She studied the road ahead, thinking. "It's a habit. Not one of my better ones. I'm constantly misplacing things."

"You said Helene became impatient at the end of lunch. Was it after you came back from the bathroom?"

"Yes," she replied, then remembered. "Actually, she had already paid for lunch and stood when I came to the table. She handed me my keys and phone. Then jokingly she told me not to lose them." She jerked her gaze to his. "You don't think—"

"The hell I don't," he answered. "Where are your keys?"

"In the ignition of my car. At the bottom of the bay."

Chapter Nine

The Victorian mansion stood five levels high. Anything less would seem impoverished to a United States senator, Frank Sweeney thought derisively. And D'Agostini was anything but impoverished. A sophisticated blend of old and new, the mansion boasted an embassy-sized ballroom, an art gallery, a wine bistro and a media room with an adjoining twenty-seat cinema.

All with coffered ceilings and herringbone floors. All tastefully gilded, draped and cosseted by one man's wealth and affluence.

But Frank wasn't here to see D'Agostini. He ignored the bodyguards flanking the entryway and the nearby elevator. Instead, temper had him climbing the grand staircase. Each jarring step increased the tempo of the hammers that beat the inside of his skull and added to his sense of self-punishment.

He'd screwed up. He hadn't anticipated the kick from the girl. Whether he wanted to admit it or not, the sight of Lomax standing in the doorway caught him off guard.

The third floor opened into a wide lobby. With quick strides, Frank walked to the far end where two oversized mahogany doors stood. Not bothering to knock, he opened the doors quietly, already hearing the battle that went on from the other side and not wanting to disturb it.

At one time, the gymnasium stood as a ballroom, now renovated into a modern miniature health club. While the vaulted ceiling remained, the walls were covered with mirrors, the hardwood floor with mats. Weights and machines flanked one side, while a bar, sauna and hot tub stood opposite.

In the middle, he saw Kragen take a short jab to his mouth. His sweat-darkened hair plastered to his head. His teeth gleamed white as he wiped blood from his lip with the back of his knuckle.

"All right, Tomas." He taunted his opponent and waved the other man forward with his fingers. "Come on."

Frank knew the instructor—a wiry martial arts expert—was left no other choice. And he had to give the man credit for taking that step forward. Mistake or not, Tomas drew blood, setting the tone for the workout. No apologies would be accepted.

Both fighters were of equal height, and equal in build. A good match for workouts. Tomas attacked with a right roundhouse kick to Kragen's face. At the last moment, Kragen sidestepped, grabbed the man's ankle and slammed his elbow into his opponent's face. Frank heard the bone crunch against cartilage, saw the blood gush.

But Frank knew Kragen wasn't finished. A second later, Kragen twisted the leg. This time, the bone snapped and Tomas screamed. Kragen followed his opponent's momentum and slammed Tomas's head into the floor. "I think we're done for the day, don't you?"

When Tomas nodded, Kragen left the man rolling in agony on the mat.

Frank opened the door, waved the guards in and watched them carry Tomas out. A dislocated knee is a small price to pay for keeping one's life.

"You keep going through instructors like that, you won't have anyone to tear apart when you really get angry," Frank commented.

"I told him I had a meeting later with the

senator. He failed to pull his punch." Oliver wiped his lip again, then grabbed a towel from the edge of the mat and patted his face.

After a moment, he studied Frank's bruised features. "It appears that I fared better than you, Frank." He threw the towel back onto the mat and walked over to the bar. "I see you found Lomax," he commented, smiling. "Or did Webber do that to you?"

Frank snorted, but took the insult. He deserved it after all. "Webber's dead."

"Really?" Oliver's smile thinned. He reached under the bar and pulled a bottle of juice from the refrigerator. "Did you finally get a stomachful or did Lomax kill him?"

"Lomax," Frank admitted. "But he only beat me by a few seconds."

"What happened?"

"I found blood on the woman's floor, suspected it was Lomax's. Before I could question the woman, Webber hit her. Pissed me off. Took my focus off of her and the situation just long enough for Lomax to catch me unaware. He burst into the room like some damn hero."

"It's not like you to blame others for your mistakes, Frank."

Frank's gaze drifted pointedly over the bar, searching.

"What are you looking for?" Kragen asked.

"Hot coffee," Frank answered, referring to Kragen's earlier meeting with Webber.

Oliver laughed and chugged some of his juice. "With your tough hide, I'd use acid," he said, but the underlying tone of truth raised the hair on the back of Frank's neck.

"The only mistake I made was not killing Webber before we even got to Grace Renne's place," Frank admitted, but the muscles in his back stayed tight. "The screwup at The Tens should have never happened."

"I agree. But then again, the senator hand-picked Webber to take care of it, didn't he?" Oliver commented dryly. "Did you take care not to leave any evidence at the Renne woman's house?"

"I did, but it wouldn't hurt to make another phone call."

"It wouldn't hurt you," Oliver said non-committally. "But the more I cover up, the more chance of exposure." He grabbed a nearby towel and hooked it around his neck. "What about Miss Renne? Is she involved?"

"Now? Definitely," Frank added, thinking of the small plastic case in his pocket.

"What about the father?"

"We're still uncertain. Webber said he'd shot Lomax. The blood I found was obviously from his wound," Sweeney said carefully. "But it couldn't have been serious. The Lomax I saw looked healthy enough. Although, his face is banged up a bit. If I had to guess, I'd say the father wasn't a problem. But he might be part of our solution."

"Webber is dead and Lomax is gone. Neither will please the senator," Kragen advised. "If we decide to pressure a prominent Washington physician, it had better be for a good reason."

"Show the senator this," Frank reached into his pocket, pulled out the miniature DVD case and handed it to Kragen. "I think you'll have your reason."

Chapter Ten

The sun had faded into the ember-orange blur of a cloudy Chesapeake dusk. In the distance, herons swooped and fed from the bay waters, their long, white bodies graceful, their eerie calls mournful.

The evening breeze picked up enough that the ends of her hair tickled her shoulders, touching off a chill that skittered down her spine. Grace stepped from the truck and hugged her arms to her chest to fight another bout of shivers.

The air was thick with the smell of pine and earth—and heavy enough with moisture that she could taste a hint of rain at the back of her throat.

Her jeans, damp and stiff, chafed against her skin with each step forward, but she ignored the discomfort.

"Not what I expected." Jacob observed from behind her, startling her.

"I think that's why you liked it," Grace admitted slowly, her heart still up in her throat.

Positioned out over the water, the four-story home stood on stilts of steel and cement. The design shouldn't have worked amongst four acres of wood, beach and bay. But it did.

The sleek, straight-lined style defined contemporary architecture with its square yet modern windows and a lone tower resting comfortably on the flat roof. Only the occasional right angle kept the design from being too boxy and gave the home enough class to be unique, not boring.

"Most homes around here are more traditional," she said, breaking through the silence that had settled between them. At one time, she'd foolishly dreamed of living here with Jacob. "Tell me again why we are here and not chasing down my keys?"

"We're going to wait until the city fishes the car out of the water. Let them do the hard work."

"How long do you think that will be?"

"Considering that we parked the car in the middle of a boat channel, I would say relatively soon," Jacob commented, slanting her a sardonic look. "And if we're lucky, they'll take the car to city impound."

"So we start making calls to find out where we go looking. Then we break in later tonight?" The shivers rippled through her. She hugged her arms to her chest to keep them contained.

"There's no we," Jacob acknowledged. "You're not going, Grace."

"Why?"

"You're pregnant," he snapped.

"And you've got a bum shoulder and no memory. That's more of a disadvantage than being pregnant if we run into a bad guy or two."

"If I don't think, my reflexes take over. Like they did at your house with Sweeney."

"That doesn't mean—"

"What happened with Sweeney and the car chase should tell you they're not going to stop. Hell, you're lucky that baby didn't get harmed when we took our dip in the bay."

"He's tougher than he looks. And so am I," she said, but she had thought the same thing and shivered once more. But this time it wasn't from the cold.

"Well, you scared the hell out of me," he replied, his voice tight. "Once we get to my place, you're going to stay put until I figure out what is going on."

"Jacob, I'd go insane waiting for some faceless predator to hunt me down in a dark corner."

"It wouldn't be a dark corner. It will be a whole different country if I have anything to say about it."

"You don't think they'd find me?"

"Not before I'd find them," he growled. "And that's a promise."

"No."

"You have no choice." His eyes snapped to hers.

"There's always a choice." Stubbornness set her jaw, but fury had her grinding her teeth.

"Why didn't you tell me you were pregnant?"

More than anything she had wanted to tell him. Had come here to his house looking to do just that and found it deserted. Her heart bled just enough to remind her she wasn't immune to the hurt yet. Better a baby without a father than a baby with a father who remained distant.

A lesson Grace learned from her own childhood.

"Because I was trying to avoid this argument," she snapped. "We have no idea who is behind this. At least with you, there's a chance you might remember."

"And the baby?" When she didn't answer, he continued, "Are you willing to put your baby at risk?"

"My baby is already at risk," she answered, pushing back the fear and doubts that threatened to suffocate her. She swiped at an annoying strand of hair that clung damply to her cheek. "Whoever gunned down Helene is still out there. I wouldn't be here right now if you had left me at my house. I'd be lying on the floor beaten and bloody from Webber's fists," she insisted, touching the sore spot on her lip with her tongue. "Even if I thought to hide at that point, he changed my mind. Nowhere is safe for me or my baby until we get to the bottom of this."

He was angry. She saw it in his features. But rather than scare her, it surprised her. The Jacob she knew never lost control, never gave anything away. This man wasn't covering up any of his emotions.

"Damn it." He pinched his nose between his thumb and forefinger. "Tell me, did I ever get the last word with you?"

"Yes. One time," she murmured. But he had to walk out on her to do it, she thought grimly. She turned her head away from him, stared out over the water until the tears stopped pricking her eyes.

"Well, the argument must have been pretty insignificant, then."

"You thought so."

"What the hell is that supposed to mean?"

"Nothing." Her tone was clipped, more out of annoyance with herself than him. "Look, I'm sorry. You don't deserve me taking shots at you."

"Just because I don't remember it doesn't mean I didn't deserve it. Either tell me what I did or wait until I gain a point of reference for the hostility. All right?"

"Yes." She watched him for a moment, saw the set of his jaw hadn't relaxed. "But I want your word, Jacob, that you won't leave me behind."

He gave her a long, considering look. "You have it."

Until the old Jacob returned, she thought. "Fine," she said, but with much less conviction.

"How are we going to get in?" She followed him over the graveled driveway to the front porch.

"Don't suppose I keep a spare set of keys under a nearby flower pot?"

"You're not the type," she mused. His sense of humor hit her with a rush of pleasure. Enough that she almost forgot their reason for being there.

Almost.

"Can you pick the lock or something?"

"Actually, I'm doing the 'or something' part." He ran his hand down around the reinforced steel door until his fingers located the security trigger. "The mechanism is too sophisticated. I don't have the right tools. A problem I'm going to have to correct soon enough." He pulled out his gun, checked the clip before placing it back in his waistband. "We seem pretty isolated. How close is my nearest neighbor?"

"My best guess would be a mile in either direction. Why?"

"Because I have a pretty damn good security system, but not a linked one."

"You mean, no police are going to show up on your door step if you trigger the alarm."

"Exactly. And if I trigger it, you might have to cover your ears. I don't expect an alarm to activate, but it's only a guess. Either way, you're not to move from the front door. No matter what. I don't want to shoot you by mistake. Got it?"

"Yes."

Without thinking, he leaned down and kissed her on the lips. A quick butterfly brush of the lips. "For luck."

Grace went still, paralyzed. Not from the touch of his mouth against hers, but from the longing the simple gesture invoked.

"I've done that before, haven't I?"

A simple gesture that gutted her from rib to belly. Grace tried to answer, tried to nod but managed neither.

He grabbed her arm, just above the elbow, shook it. "Tell me."

She managed a short nod then, but the words took another second to push past the tightening in her throat. "It was somewhat of a ritual you did when you left on one of your business trips."

She saw the shift, the laser sharpness that entered his gaze. Knew the rejection, the long-ago hurt showed in hers.

"Hell." He muttered the curse even as he dropped his hand. "Stay here. Don't move."

For a moment, she watched him melt into the semidarkness and almost laughed. Would have if she could have been sure hysteria didn't spur the urge.

Leave, he said? She took a deep, shuddering

breath, realizing hysterics weren't so far-fetched.

Just where in the hell was she supposed to go?

FATIGUE RODE HIM HARD, making his movements slower, more sluggish than he would've liked. But it was the rage, the frustration over Grace's pain that drove him deeper into the shadows. That and the sweet taste of her still lingering on his lips.

Jacob worked his way around the perimeter of the house, stopping every few steps to listen, to wait. The wind rustled the trees, making the leaves dance and the branches whistle. In the background, the water rushed the beach, slapping foam and grit against the rocks in its path.

She'd stood her ground against Webber, he'd give her that. Held her own in a car chase, too. With five cops on her tail. Hell, she even managed to take down Sweeney without Jacob's help.

He played the last through his mind in slow motion. Damn, he thought he'd lost her that time. All it would've taken is one of Sweeney's meaty hands squeezing her neck.

His scowl brought a sharp tug of pain from the stitches in his forehead. He'd get her into the house, then he'd get some answers.

As darkness settled in, his eyes adjusted. He quickly discovered his night vision worked well enough for him to place most shadows into decipherable patterns.

From what he could see, there were no thermal or motion detectors. Considering the house sat on the edge of the woods, he wasn't surprised. Too many deer to hinder that kind of security.

Soundlessly, he worked his way to the back, noting the freestanding generator, two satellite dishes and a series of solar panels.

It seemed the house was set up to be independent of outside sources. The simplest way to maintain anonymity, if that was one's goal.

Considering they were two miles off the nearest main road, intentional isolation had been a distinct possibility.

Toward the back, he discovered the attached garage housing an SUV and a black Mercedes. Both locked up tight.

It wasn't until he investigated the boat dock, that he felt a deep pull of satisfaction in his belly. Wide enough to house two boats, the dock sat snuggly underneath the stilts of the house.

He sure as hell hit the jackpot.

The prize? A midnight-black Malibu speedboat moored to the steel posts—its keys still in the ignition.

ONE MINUTE STRETCHED to five, then ten. Agitation worked Grace's nerves until she was forced to pace back and forth to ease her anxiety. In the dark, the shadows seemed to grow and stretch. But it wasn't the shadows that left her on edge.

"Grace."

She screamed, swung around and realized too late that it was Jacob who stood in the doorway behind her.

He caught her fist with a smack against his palm.

"Damn it," she swore, more at herself for being jumpy. "Make some noise when you walk up behind me."

Inside the door, a security box buzzed. He dropped her hand, then reached over and broke open the box with the gun. He ripped out the inner wires.

The buzzing stopped.

"How did you get in?"

"Through a back window," he answered, tossing the lid onto the floor. "I broke the pane with the butt of my gun."

"It was that easy?"

"Not quite."

"But what if they come here?"

"There are other ways to protect us." He shot her a sardonic look. "Besides, if everything else fails—" the cold-blue of his eyes flickered to his weapon "—this seems to work well enough."

"Until it runs out of bullets," she retorted before following him through the doorway.

He shut the door behind them and turned the dead bolt. But made no other move. Instead, he leaned back against the door and folded his arms.

He glanced at the ceiling. "Lights on."

Track lights flipped on, hurting his eyes.

"Lights eighty percent capacity."

The relief was minimal, but acceptable. "How did you know to say that particular phrase?"

"I didn't think about it." The harshness of the light emphasized the unyielding lines of his features. "I think it's time you and I had a discussion."

"Jacob, I'm tired—"

"It's called, 'she said, he believed.' And it won't take long," he continued, ignoring her gasp of protest. "She said they were friends. He believed they were lovers."

"This is ridiculous," she replied, striving for nonchalance, but the small quiver in her voice and his raised eyebrow told her she'd failed.

"She said the baby she carried was another man's. He believed it was his."

Suddenly in two quick strides, he was in front of her. His hands gripped her shoulders, preventing her retreat. "She said he left with no goodbye. And for no reason."

Her head tilted back. "And?" she whispered, torn. "What did he believe?"

"There was no goodbye. But no reason?" he murmured as one hand slid up the back of her neck, cupping her head with enough pressure to bring her up against him. Her fingers curled into his sweater, holding her there suspended. "There had to be one hell of a reason for me to walk away from you."

His free arm slid around her, curving her body into his. Giving her only a second to adjust to the heat, to accept the primal intent that set his features into hard lines.

Then his mouth was on hers. But not with the fierceness she had expected. Certainly not with the same fierceness that her heart beat in her chest or the blood pounded through her veins.

His lips settled into a persuasive tempo that swept her up, rolled her under, left her trying to find her feet under their tender assault.

Caution tugged at her, urging her to step back. But the warmth of his body, the stroke of his hand up her spine blurred her thoughts, spiked her emotions until her arms slid up and around his neck.

With a groan, he deepened the kiss. He used his tongue to coax her mouth open. Then used it again to reward her, when her lips parted. Stroking, tasting.

A yearning broke free, snapping through her, catching her in a backlash of need. To be held, comforted. Cherished.

With a cry, she pushed away. Humiliation coursed through her, its ugly head rearing up, sniping at her soul, making her nauseous.

"Grace?"

Tears burned her eyes, but she blinked them back. She put out a hand, stopping him from grabbing her again.

"Please don't."

His arms dropped to his sides, but his hands became fists. The shadows cut edges into his already sharp features, turned his eyes into hard blue stones. "Tell me, damn it."

She understood what he was asking. First with his kiss, now with the words. Stricken with embarrassment, she clung to the one thing that straightened her spine, hitched her chin and locked her eyes on his. Self-preservation.

"This baby is not yours."

Chapter Eleven

"If I'm not the father, who is, Grace?"

"My baby doesn't have a father. Not in the sense you mean, anyway." Her eyes burned— from fatigue or the tears, she couldn't be sure. She rubbed them gently with her fingertips. "Besides, I met him after you left, so you never knew him."

"Did you tell him?"

"No," she said, using that part of the truth as her defense. "He isn't father material."

"Compared to whom?"

"I guess to my own." She sighed, suddenly so weary her bones ached with it. Lord, why couldn't he have forgotten his stubbornness along with his memory? "Look, Jacob. I don't want to be analyzed. Not tonight. Okay?"

"Fair enough," he bit out, exasperated.

She glanced around, striving for a lightness she didn't feel. "The house hasn't changed since I've been here."

"How long ago was that?"

"Four months," she answered, but didn't explain the reason. Jacob didn't push her. Instead, he studied his home. If you could call it that, he noted dryly.

Exceptionally renovated, the main floor was laid out in a wide, airy space. The entrance-way opened into a two-story living room with a loft and a black mahogany circular stairway that led from the boat dock beneath and to the third level above.

"Looks like I kept a pretty simple existence." Jacob looked around, trying to find something familiar.

Paintings covered the walls—expensive, judging from the vivid colors and the broad strokes. His tastes obviously ran toward abstract and modern, he thought, eyeing a particular flamboyant red and blue bust of a naked woman over the inset fireplace.

"The word is *impersonal*," Grace commented quietly.

Quiet, he noted with growing admiration, not cowed.

"Do you realize that while you don't necessarily know my history, you really do seem to know me?"

"That's not true—"

"You know I like my coffee black," he pointed out. "What else do you know?"

"Nothing, really." She paused. "Maybe little things."

"So if you had to guess, what would be my favorite color?"

"Black," she answered, using her hand to sweep over the room. "Most things you own are black. Your cars. Your clothes. Your boat. Even your furniture."

"That's gloomy, isn't it?"

"You told me once it kept you from having to worry about coordinating problems."

"Seriously?"

"No, you winked at the time. But now that I think back on it, there might be some truth there."

"And my favorite music?"

For the first time she realized she did know many things about the man. Maybe not what he did for a living or about his background and family. But the man himself. Why hadn't she realized that before?

"Jazz. Blues. Rock—most of the vintage, less of the contemporary. And wine. You built a wine cellar to hold a pretty extensive and quite expensive collection."

"I'll have to try a little later," he mused. "Go on."

Grace shifted until she could see his profile, giving in to the sudden urge to study his expression while she gave him details. "You have a small addiction for a good cigar. One that you rarely indulge. A bigger addiction to fast cars—which you indulge frequently. You like five-star hotels, secluded tables in restaurants and are always willing to pay the money for good service."

"So I'm a big tipper."

"One of the biggest I've ever met," she teased. "*Huge* tips."

He gave her an exaggerated frown. "That's hard to believe."

"You don't play into the metrosexual trend and wouldn't be caught dead getting a manicure. But a good, deep massage by an attractive woman's another story. You'd keep it professional, but why turn down good eye candy while you're relaxing?"

Jacob got the distinct impression she was teasing him, but instinctively he knew better than to pursue it. For the first time, he'd gotten her to open up and he didn't want to spoil the mood. "Anything else?"

"You've told me details about countries that only someone well traveled would know. And as you said, you speak several different languages. I've heard French, Spanish and Mandarin."

"Sounds like I'm well rounded if you add in the weapons training." He stopped just short of sarcasm.

Her features softened into uncertain lines. "One time, you mentioned your mother."

"What was she like?"

"You didn't say," she replied, shrugging her shoulders. "You just told me that she would've liked me. But I don't think you meant to."

A pang of regret shot through Jacob, catching him off guard. He searched for an image or memory of his mom. A whispered word that would remind him of her voice, but it was a futile effort. "The one aspect of amnesia I never expected to deal with were the echoes of emotion."

"I don't understand."

"I had figured from the beginning that bits of my past would come back to me a little at a time or in one sweeping rush," he acknowledged. "But it's the emotions that are taking the jabs at me."

When Grace didn't say anything, Jacob

glanced her way. But her face was turned from him. "What is it?'

When her eyes found his again, there was a sadness there. "It's just you've never said anything like that to me before. You never shared your thoughts."

"Maybe that will change," he said quietly before shifting his attention back to their surroundings. "I took a quick look around on my way to the front door. One bedroom. No office. If I'm a businessman, why wouldn't I have an office here? Or somewhere?"

"You told me once you never felt the need to have an office."

"No office. Sterile living quarters. Weapons and language expert. Doesn't seem I'm adding up to be an everyday Joe, does it?" Jacob glanced at the sleek black cabinets and hi-tech appliances. "Do I like to cook?"

"Not really. So I guess we can rule out chef,"

she answered and ran her hand over the granite top. "But you once told me you had an associate who loved to cook, so you kept your kitchen stocked for him."

"No name?"

"None."

Grace slid onto the bar stool next to the counter.

"Are you okay?"

Grace nodded. "Just tired." Exhausted really, but she didn't want to give him another reason to hold her. Comfort her. Not while her nerves were still snapping from their last encounter.

He studied her for a moment. "My fault," he murmured, the words more of a caress than an apology. The pleasure from them shot through her, an arrow to the belly. One that left her insides more than a little quivery.

"Why don't you get out of those clothes and

take a shower. I want to check around the house some more, anyway. See if I can find anything that might prod my memory."

A shower sounded wonderful. Just what she needed to shake the chill from her bones, wash the feel of him from her skin. But she could wait. "Actually, I think we should change your bandage. See how much damage you've done."

"All right. But let's at least change our clothes. I'm sure we can find something warm to wear in the bedroom. Then you can change my bandage." He grabbed her hand and tugged her up the stairs behind him. When they reached the master bedroom, Jacob walked to the closet.

"Helene's?" He nodded to a row of dresses hanging on the rod.

"Yes." Startled, her eyes skimmed the pile of chiffon and sequins. "She moved in a few months back. About a month after you left."

Slowly, she picked out a black sarong evening gown. "I've seen her wear most of these dresses."

"Were she and I lovers?"

"Maybe at one time, but it would've been long before I met her or you." Grace frowned, trying to remember Helene over the last few weeks. "Actually, she was never involved with anyone seriously."

"Even lately?"

"I don't know. If there was, I never met him," she said. "Helene went through men pretty quickly." Grace studied Jacob. "She might have told you."

"Which doesn't help at all," he commented, then sorted through some of his clothes on the opposite side.

Moments later, Jacob scanned the bedroom. He took in the crisp, clean lines of the platform bed. With drapes and linens of tan and the sleeker base of black wood—nothing else was needed to highlight the masculine edge.

"Do you recognize anything?"

"No." His eyes followed the curved stairway in the corner. Of the whole house, this was his favorite feature. An exclusive access to the tower room on the roof.

"If I was hiding papers, I'd want them close and protected. I'd want to be able to grab and go." His eyes worked their way around the walls. "Something hidden in plain sight."

"Would it be small or big?"

"Small. Travel light." The disconnection gnawed at him. "But it wouldn't be in here. Too obvious."

Grace laid her hand on his forearm and squeezed. "Give it time."

"We don't have time." He tugged his hand

free, not liking the empathy behind the words, not when somewhere deep inside he wanted more than that from her.

Fatigue paled her porcelain skin, left dark smudges beneath her eyes. "Look, why don't you get dressed first? I'm sure you can find something here. Meanwhile, I want to take another look at my boat."

A smile tugged at the corners of her mouth. "That boat was your baby."

"Might still be," he responded, a small grin of his own tugged at his mouth. "After, I'll take another turn around the perimeter before it gets dark."

"Perimeter?" Grace asked. "That's military, isn't it?"

"Goes with the weapons training, I imagine," he answered. "Go change. I'll be back before you know it."

Without thought, he went to gather her close.

An automatic instinct to comfort. But just as quickly, she sidestepped him, placing more than a few feet of distance between them.

"Don't." The word wasn't a plea or an order. A hint of desperation underlined it. Enough that he couldn't even be sure she directed the statement solely at him. "All right?"

Jacob stiffened, finally understanding. The fear had never been of him or that he might harm her again. Although, in his mind, he must have certainly warranted it.

No, she feared herself—or her reaction, he corrected. She didn't trust herself.

He watched her leave the room, not waiting for his reply. A good thing, since he had no intention of answering her.

Not yet, anyway.

GRACE STEPPED OUT of the bathroom a half hour later feeling refreshed and in control once again. She'd found Helene's emerald-green velour jogging suit and decided it would be perfect for pajamas. Helene was one size larger than Grace, but that worked in Grace's favor. She rolled down the waist until it hung low on her hips and gave some relief on her stomach.

"You look comfortable."

Grace stopped midstride and glanced up. Jacob stood across the room wearing nothing more than a worn pair of jeans.

"So do you." He was barefooted and bare-chested. The dim glow of the bedroom light surrounded him, softening the harsh bruises and the white gauze of his bandage, shadowing the lean, hard form of his chest and the sleek, tight muscles of his arms.

Her gaze traveled down the masculine contours of his ribs, drawn like a moth to the flickering light that danced over the taut skin of his belly. Her mouth went dry as she followed the line of sable hair that started slightly below his navel and disappeared into the open vee of his unsnapped waistband.

"Are you ready?"

"I'm sorry?" Grace forced her eyes upward and caught the slight flexing of his jaw muscles, telling her he hadn't missed her perusal.

"I asked if you were ready to change my bandage," he repeated, but each word was low, raspy. Each syllable ground against the next, sandpaper on sandpaper.

"Yes." She forced herself to take a long, steady breath.

"I found this in the boat." He grabbed a first aid kit from the bed and held it up. "Are you sure you're up for this? The wound isn't going to be pretty."

"It's nothing I haven't seen before," she

managed, forcing her legs to walk toward him. "Who do you think took care of you before my father got to my house?" When Jacob raised his eyebrow, she added, "I was premed when I dropped out of college."

"Okay, Doc." Jacob nodded toward the bathroom. "I'm all yours."

She waited a moment to get her heartbeat under control, then followed him in.

Jacob sat on the bathroom counter, putting his shoulder eye level for Grace.

Grace murmured her apologies, concentrated on cutting away the bandage. Soon she was finished, and she took a deep breath.

"How does it look?"

"The wound is crusted with dried blood, but otherwise the sutures are still intact."

She dipped a clean washcloth into some water from the sink and started to wash away the blood.

"Tell me about your mom," Jacob said softly.

Because it kept her mind off their proximity, she obliged him. "Her name was Claire. She met my father during the Vietnam War. She worked for Senator Langdon, although he was a colonel then."

"And your father?"

"He was an army surgeon. The way my father tells the story, my mom came in to deliver some papers and it was love at first sight." She laid the wet towel down and used another to pat his wound dry. "They were married a little over twelve years when she died."

"How?"

"She was in a plane crash with Senator Langdon. He was seeking reelection."

Ignoring the slight trembling in her fingers, she applied some antibiotic cream.

"You must look like her."

She opened the package of square bandages,

pulled one out and placed it against his wound. "Yes. Very much so." Carefully, she taped the bandage down.

Jacob's fingers played with a thick lock of her hair, testing its weight, the texture. The scent so familiar, something inside him strained to break free. "Honeysuckle," he murmured, reining the emotion back as her fingers fluttered and stroked him. Not with the heat of passion, but with the softness of concern.

"I'm sorry?" She shifted closer in order to start wrapping the gauze over his bicep first.

"Your shampoo is called Honeysuckle Sweet. When I remembered the trip to Aspen, it was because I recognized the scent of your hair. I looked in your bathroom when I couldn't remember the name of the flower."

"The fact that you noticed surprises me." Her gaze snapped to his. A moment later, she noticed how the dampness of the bay and wind clung to him. How the scent enticed her to lean in closer. "I didn't mean that in a rude way."

"I understand," he said, the truth of it saddening his words. "Maybe I didn't then. Who knows? But I'm noticing a lot of things now, Grace." He rubbed the strands of her hair between his thumb and forefinger. "Why is it I can remember the texture and scent of your hair, but nothing else?"

"Maybe because I was the last person you saw before you passed out." She saw the flash in his eyes, the desire that took the blue to slate. Her hand went to his chest to hold him off, but she ended up curling her fingers in the soft hair.

"My memories revolve around scents. Textures." His finger slid down her cheek, settled at the corner of her mouth. "Tastes."

Her body shuddered at the images his words invoked. "Stop, Jacob."

"I've tasted you before." His lips replaced his finger trailing down her cheek to the hollow beneath her ear. He nibbled, groaning softly when her body jerked in reaction. "Sweet." His mouth followed the line of her throat. Her head tilted back giving him more access. "Help me remember, Grace."

The heat of his mouth licked over her skin, seeped into her pores. Help him remember? She couldn't even think. Couldn't breathe.

The heat became dizzying. She reached out, tried to hold on. Suddenly, Jacob broke off the kiss. He swore. It wasn't until then she noticed her hand gripping his shoulder.

Fear made her drop her hand, but it was embarrassment that made her take a step back.

"Well, nothing like a little pain to kill the mood." Jacob strained for light humor, but couldn't get it past the rasp in his throat.

"No more," she whispered on a shaky breath. Her eyes darted to his. "I won't be seduced—"

"Again?" He shrugged and moved off the counter. "All right. We won't go there. For now."

When he stepped out of the bathroom, she found herself following him. "I mean it," she insisted, even if the words sounded lame to her own ears.

"All right." He tugged on a dress shirt, buttoned it half way up. "I could use something to eat. How about you?" When she didn't answer, he continued, "We only have a few hours before we go after your keys. I suggest you eat something, then take a nap." When he walked past her, he kissed her gently on the forehead. "You look like hell, Grace."

"I what?" But her words fell on an empty room. Annoyed, she followed him into the kitchen.

"There's milk, eggs, an assortment of take-out leftovers." Jacob straightened from inside the refrigerator.

"The house looks hardly lived in."

"You've always had a cleaning service—" Grace froze.

"What is it?"

"I've figured out a way to call my father."

"No," he declared. "The authorities will be watching your father."

"He has a housekeeper. Her name is Carol Reed. The police wouldn't have tapped into her cell phone, right?"

"Probably not, but that doesn't mean—"

"I can call her—"

"I said *probably,* Grace," he emphasized. "Even if the police overlooked her phone, would you trust her not to report back to them?"

"Yes. She's been with my father for years."

"It's too much of a risk," he said after a moment.

"If he's talked to the police, he might be able to help us," she pressed.

"It's still too risky. There's equipment out there. Laser microphones, for instance. A good one will pick up conversations from a hundred yards away."

"A what?"

"A microphone that…" He shoved his fingers through his hair. "Never mind."

"If I promise to not give out any information, we should be safe. Right?"

"What if Helene's murderers have a tap on your dad? What makes you think they won't use him to get to you? If you're not worried about your safety, worry about his."

"I am. That's why I want to warn him, Jacob." Her statement drifted between them. A hushed whisper filled with fear.

Jacob swore. "All right. Is his house fairly large? Bigger than this one?"

"Yes."

"Then have him walk into the closet or another room without windows."

"Why?"

"If they haven't bugged the house or the phones, they would have to use a laser microphone, which needs a window to record voice vibrations."

"These are big 'ifs.'"

Jacob handed her a disposable phone. "Make it short, simple. And no information. You can tell him you're safe. Even tell him not to worry. But don't tell him anything else. Then hang up."

"He might have information." She punched Carol's number into the phone.

"Then he better give it to you quickly. No more than a minute, Grace."

The phone picked up after the first ring.

"Hello?"

"Carol, it's Grace." She heard the house-keeper gasp, pictured her small, round face going slack with shock. "Please don't say my name out loud. And listen for a moment. I need you to go to the nearest room without window. A bathroom or a closet, okay?"

"Okay. One moment."

"Thank you, Carol." She waited until she heard a door shut. "Where are you?"

"In the pantry." Carol paused, seemingly shaking off her upset. "Grace. My god, where are you? Your father is sick with worry."

"I know," she replied, grateful the house-keeper had followed her instructions. "Tell me. Have the police been there?"

"Not the police. But someone from the government. FBI maybe," Carol answered, her voice lowered to a whisper. "They did not talk to me, so I can't be sure. But they spent over an hour in the library with your father."

"Is he there?"

"Yes. He hasn't left since he discovered you missing at your home."

"I'm going to hang up, Carol. I want you to get my dad and make sure he stays in the pantry with your phone. Tell him I'll ring him in five minutes. Okay?"

"Okay, Grace," the older woman acknowledged. "I don't know what you're involved in, but please take care of yourself."

"I will. Thank you." Grace hung up the phone before the housekeeper responded.

For the next five minutes, Grace paced the floor. Neither she nor Jacob spoke but the hard set of his features told her he wasn't happy.

Finally, Grace hit the phone's redial.

Her father answered on the first ring.

"Grace?"

"Hi, Dad." She paced back and forth, ignoring Jacob's frown.

"Thank God. Are you okay. Are you safe?"

"I'm safe," she answered. "Are you in the pantry, Dad?"

"Yes, yes," he said impatiently. "Where are you? When I got back to your house I found—"

"I know what you found. Look, I don't have much time," she said. "Have you been questioned by the police?"

"Of course. I walked right into their crime scene," he answered. "Why did you run away?"

"Dad, those two men tried to kill us. They broke into the house—"

"There were two?"

"Yes, Jacob knocked the second unconscious."

"Grace," Jacob warned, his hand reaching for the phone. She jerked away.

"Grace, where are you?"

"I told you, somewhere safe." She glanced at Jacob.

"Come home. The police can protect you."

"No. These men are dangerous, Dad. I think they have connections. Until I'm sure, I need you to be careful."

"The police think you're dead. Murdered by the same person who killed Helene," her father said, his tone low, suspicious. "They suspect it's Jacob."

"Did you tell them he was there?"

"No. But if they search hard enough, they'll probably turn up his DNA." Her father paused. "Is Jacob Lomax the baby's father?"

"Yes."

Her father swore. Something he never did. "Dad—"

"Never mind that, Grace. They questioned me about Helene's computer. Do you have it? They said it wasn't in the office or her home. They seem to think it holds the key to her murder."

"I don't have it. I thought it was at the bar."

"Grace," Jacob prompted.

"I've got to go, Dad. Please be careful. These men are dangerous," she whispered, blinking back tears. Words caught like shards of glass, shredding her throat until it burned like hellfire. She hung up the phone.

"I couldn't say it." Tears formed, then spilled. "I couldn't tell my own father that I love him."

Suddenly, Jacob's arms were around her. He led her to the couch and cradled her in his lap.

And she cried. Long, gut-wrenching sobs that set her body quaking. The problem was, she didn't know what she was crying over. Helene. The baby. Her father.

She cried because, at that moment, she had no more left in her. No more courage. No more strength.

Nothing left but the need to release.

For what seemed like hours, Jacob held her. Rocking her close to his chest. And when that didn't work, he whispered soothing words against her temple.

When the tears stopped and she settled, he kissed the wetness off her cheeks, rubbed her back until the shaking stopped.

"Feel better?"

She nodded into the hollow of his neck. "I don't suppose we can blame my hormones for that?"

His laugh rumbled deep within his chest. She tucked her hands between their chests, used his heartbeat to soothe.

"I'd probably blame exhaustion myself."

"I can see your point. A good cry is always draining." Her lips curved into a smile against his throat. "I'll tell you what. When it's your turn for a bout of hysteria, I'll hold you. Then after, we'll blame yours on the hormones."

"Deal." He shifted, reclining back on the couch. He pulled her down to him, tucking her head beneath his chin, her legs caught between his. "I think we both could use a nap."

She snuggled her cheek against the open vee of his shirt, enjoying the clean, masculine scent, the comforting rhythm of his heart beneath her cheek.

She'd missed this. The closeness with another human being. The simple act of holding someone, touching him, comforting him.

Loving him.

The crying, she understood now, had been the catalyst she needed to clear her head, help her mind catch up to what her heart already understood.

She'd never fallen out of love with Jacob.

Chapter Twelve

"We should have made the eleven o'clock news," Jacob commented while Grace cleared away their dinner dishes.

She'd woken up earlier to the sizzle of bacon and eggs frying.

"Guess the murder wasn't as big a deal as we thought," she said wryly.

"Or instead of the police covering up," Jacob answered, his brows lowered into a frown, "someone in the media is stopping it. Or both."

"You're saying that whoever is involved in

Helene's murder owns the media in this area?"

"It's a definite possibility."

A chill went down Grace's spine.

"Tell me about Helene."

Grace wiped her hands on a nearby dish towel and leaned against the counter. "No-nonsense. Sexy in a cool, untouchable way. You were very much alike. You could have been formed from the same mold. A his and hers. I think I envied that about both of you."

"How did you meet?"

"At a political event. I was dating an up-and-coming lobbyist at the time."

"Was she political then?"

"Yes. Extremely so. Very much like my father. She enjoyed living amongst the Capitol Hill elite. Especially lately."

"Why do you say that?"

"The presidential election is only a few

months away and she had been following the coverage very closely. She always seemed connected to everything. Politics, business, the world economy. She attended the right dinner parties, always escorted by the right people."

"You sound like you envied her."

"Only her decisiveness. She had the courage to back up her choices."

"From where I'm sitting, she has nothing on you."

"You wouldn't say that if you remembered her," she prodded mildly.

"Maybe she considered you her friend."

"She did. I think you and I were her closest, and still I didn't know much about her," Grace replied. "And now she's dead and I don't even know who to notify."

"Did she have a safe? Anything that she kept her personal papers in?"

"None that I knew." Grace stopped, slapped

her hands on the counter in quick succession. "That's wrong. She kept most of her business records on her computer. One of those new, sleek laptops."

Grace swung to him. "Dad said the police were interested in finding her computer. At the time, it didn't register because I was overwhelmed emotionally. But he said the police couldn't find the laptop at the bar or her apartment."

"If she had always had it with her, it would have been at the bar, right?" Jacob glanced around. "Or here."

"Pusher." A slow smile slid across her face. "With everything going on, I forgot about Pusher."

"Who's Pusher?"

"Pusher Davis. My bar manager. Ex–bar manager." She straightened from the counter. "If I'm right, Helene had her

computer with her. She never went anywhere without it."

"So it's at the bar."

"No, Pusher has Helene's computer."

"How can you be sure?"

"Because Pusher is an ex-con." She paced
the floor, trying to sort through the steps the
bar manager would have taken after discov-
ering Helene's body.

"I'm not following."

"He's an ex-con who did time for cyber-
crimes. With a specialty or passion, I guess,
for hacking into corporate and federal
accounts. And my understanding is that he
was the best."

"So, the first thing he would've noticed
was—"

"Helene's computer." She sat on the couch,
drew up her knees. "He would've taken it.
Out of loyalty, if nothing else. Pusher hates

cops. The only thing he hates more, he says, is dirty cops."

"First, we find Pusher," Jacob reasoned. "Then we get your keys from the impound."

LAWRENCE "PUSHER" DAVIS stepped off the apartment's elevator. The red carpet, well-lit hallway and pristine chandeliers spoke high-class in volumes.

Pusher lived on the trendy side of Washington, D.C. Overblown, expensive but in the game he played, it was all about image.

The paper bag rattled a bit in his hand when he dug for his key. Because it played well to anyone happening by, he shifted the bag up into the crook of his arm like a sack of groceries.

For a moment, the irony struck him as funny. Pusher Davis carrying pretend groceries. It wasn't too long back that he'd been forced to go for days without food.

Pusher had grown up with a Baptist mother in South Texas. His father was nothing more than a temporary lover with enough cash to keep his mother in bourbon. Not that Pusher cared. His mom wasn't a mean drunk. On the contrary: the deeper into her stupors, the more genteel she became—spouting one slurred Bible verse after another until she passed out.

Until one day, she passed out and choked to death on her own vomit.

Barely ten years of age and homeless, Pusher took to the streets with only one valuable lesson—the need to survive superseded any laws of man and God.

At the age of twelve, he learned that cops held the same attitude.

And at the age of thirteen, he learned that information, of any kind, was power.

That's when he stole his first computer.

Now he was a grown man, one whom the ladies recognized as a charmer and a rogue. He kept trim, because it was expected, and his muscles were defined, not bulky, because that's what filled a tailored suit well.

He'd been born poor, but knew from the Bible that people better than him had risen from dirt. A kid on the street, he watched people. He educated himself, studying only the people others stepped out of the way for. How they walked, how they styled themselves. Some he followed for days, studying their lives from the shadows of his own. Eventually, he'd embraced the best of their qualities and shed their worst like a snake's skin.

And when he dug deep and still couldn't find what he needed, he stole it—by mimicking those he'd watched or taking advantage of the poor souls he hadn't.

He had no doubts about who and what he was, but, more importantly, about what he'd done and had become.

The rest was God given. Six feet in height, ice-blue eyes and a boy-next-door grin. Add to the package sun-kissed blond hair—groomed on the short side, styled in the trend of messy chic—and a keen mind.

He held no ill will toward his mother. In fact, he'd always thank her and the sweet Lord for giving him a Texas accent and knowledge of the Bible. Both proved irreplaceable as tools for a hi-tech con man.

Now reformed.

He smiled at the word. As much as a con man could ever reform. His talent ran toward conversation and computers. To him, that made him just an everyday businessman. After all, in his opinion, some of the best cons were pulled by businessmen.

He set Helene's computer on his desk and started it up. The fact he was breaking his parole by just carrying the laptop didn't phase him a bit. The point was just not to get caught.

As predicted, the police had run his rap sheet. He'd been dragged down to the station and questioned to all hours of the morning. Accusations were thrown back and forth between him and the cops.

He enjoyed the hell out of it. It was an enlightening meeting. Getting grilled gave Pusher a good opportunity to find out more about what was going on. Not by what was said, but more by what wasn't.

Pusher flipped on the lights and went directly to the kitchen. He grabbed a dark ale—his favorite import—from the refrigerator.

A few hours into the interrogation, it all suddenly stopped. They released him with no explanation. In fact, if he had to guess, the investigation was no longer a priority. If it made the local news, he'd be surprised.

The computer flashed on, its screen asking for the password. It would take time, but he would break it. And then he'd find what he was looking for.

Opportunity.

Chapter Thirteen

The meeting hadn't gone well. Richard D'Agostini hadn't expected it to. These men and women were the elite one percent of the world. Bankers, politicians, media moguls, royalty. They were not accustomed to failing, and now they were vulnerable. They had agreed, albeit reluctantly, to a small window of time to let him deal with the situation.

And deal with it he would.

Tall, stoic and somewhat bald, he had the older, notable features of a Harvard scholar.

And he played the distinguished, upper-class role of Senate Majority Leader like one who'd risen to royalty. He wore his pedigree like a tailored suit—custom-made and fitted, with a well-honed charm and a sense of diplomacy.

A quick knock on his suite door drew his attention. "Come in."

Oliver Kragen loosened his tie as he shut the door behind him.

"Oliver. Have a seat." Richard indicated one of the high-back leather chairs. "Do you have a situation report?"

"Lomax killed Webber," Oliver said without preamble. "Not that it was a loss."

"You mean because Webber was my man." It was a statement, not a question, but one Richard wanted answered nonetheless.

Oliver had been working for Richard for too many years not to understand his answer had better be an acceptable one.

"No, because Webber was an encumbrance. Lomax escaped from us twice because of him." Oliver sat in the chair and rested his ankle across one knee.

"He didn't allow Helene Garrett past his guard. You did." Richard paused, sensing rather than seeing Oliver's annoyance. Oliver was too good at what he did to show any reaction to Richard's baiting, but the senator couldn't help twisting the knife just a little bit more. Sometimes Oliver needed reminding of who pulled his strings. "And it seems the score now is three for Lomax, one for you." He walked over to his minibar and picked up the decanter of Scotch. "It appears Mr. Lomax is getting the better of you, Oliver."

He poured two glasses and brought one over to the younger man.

"Lomax is containable, Senator," Oliver commented, then took the glass and finished it in one swallow.

Something Richard would never consider doing. "Suppose you tell me how you plan on containing him." Richard took a drink from his glass.

"Once we have the Primoris files and the code back, he becomes less of a threat," Oliver reasoned.

"First we have to get them back."

Oliver pulled a disk from his pocket and walked over to the television. "Helene and Grace Renne had lunch together yesterday at a local bistro. Sweeney got his hands on the restaurant's security tapes. Seems the owner is somewhat of a techno nut and has a pretty decent security setup." He placed the DVD into the driver and hit the button. "Here's something you might want to see."

"You took a video from someone," the senator stated.

"Not me. Sweeney."

"At gunpoint?" Richard understood Oliver certainly wouldn't have hesitated to do the job himself. Something Richard never approved of really. As his top aide, Oliver needed to curb his tendencies toward violence.

Oliver shrugged. "Does it matter? I'm sure he was discreet."

A picture flashed across the television screen of Helene Garrett at a table, alone.

Oliver froze her image. "Take a look."

"What is she grabbing?" the senator asked as he watched, his drink held midair.

"Grace Renne's phone and keys."

"So what?" He took another swallow, then set the glass down.

"Watch." Oliver hit the slow motion button. Both men watched as Helene brought the phone and keys under the table into her lap. Two minutes later, she got up to leave.

"She kept her hands under the table," Oliver

observed. "I think Helene made the drop to Grace Renne before she even met with Lomax last night."

"Looks like someone is keeping secrets from us," Richard mused. "So are we assuming Grace Renne now knows?"

"I think we must assume that, sir,"

"Then take care of her. I want to see this over, Oliver," Richard ordered. "Now."

"It will be," Oliver agreed. "By the way, I had Lomax's DNA run through the government databases."

"And?"

"If he's an operative, the government buried him deep. One of my associates is working on it."

"It doesn't matter. Whoever he is, we'll find him," he murmured, and gazed out over the city. "And with him, we'll have the Renne woman and the Primoris file."

THE WIND PICKED UP pieces of garbage, whipped them around like confetti in front of the strip club. Its only neon light flashed its name, Chancellor's, in a hot-pink flare that drew more than the casual crowd off the street.

"Are you sure this is safe?" Grace asked.

"It's packed in here. Pusher made a good choice. Would be hard to find us in here."

"Good evening, sir." The dark eyes of the doorman—a guy on the younger side of thirty with more tattoos than hair—were curious but steady as they swept over Grace. "Club rules require that I search our guests. Do you mind?"

Grace tensed next to Jacob. He slid his arm around her and drew her close. "Not at all." Jacob smiled easily.

With a quiet efficiency, the bouncer patted Jacob down and checked Grace's purse.

"Thank you." The bouncer handed Grace

back her purse and stepped to the side. "Enjoy your visit."

After walking through the door, Grace slipped the gun from under Helene's navy peacoat and gave it to Jacob. "How did you know he wouldn't search me?"

"Educated guess."

The music was loud, the air thick with cigars and perfumed oils.

A woman appeared, her black jacket and matching miniskirt identifying her as one of the bartenders. "Mr. Lomax?"

"Yes," Jacob answered, his hand cupping Grace's elbow.

"Mr. Davis asked me to escort you to his table. This way, please."

They followed the woman to a semihidden booth in one of the far corners of the club.

"Pusher." Grace sighed in relief. She stepped away from Jacob to give her bar manager a hug. "I'm so glad to see you're okay."

Pusher pulled Grace into the curved booth beside him and kissed her cheek. "How are you doing?" His eyes darted down, just enough for her to get his meaning. She gave him another quick hug. "Fine. We're both fine."

"Lomax." Pusher rose slightly, reached across the table for a handshake. "Sure am glad to see you again."

"Glad to be seen," Jacob said noncommittally.

When Jacob didn't reach to shake, Pusher's hand dropped to his tie, smoothing it down. "Act like your having a good time. Otherwise, we're all in trouble." He waved a few fingers, signaling the waitress.

Within moments, a waitress dressed in a French maid's outfit appeared at their table. The woman was slight in build, teetering on the unhealthy side of one hundred pounds. A short cap of blond curls framed thin, delicate features, adding almost a comical edge to the slashes of red blush across each cheekbone and the matching crimson lipstick that slicked puffy lips. But it was her eyes that drew Grace's attention, caused her to settle uncomfortably in her seat. The big, sky-blue irises glittered with an unnatural intensity, rapidly shifting back and forth beneath long, mascara-laden lashes. "Hello. What can I get you all?"

Pusher smiled, revealing a perfect set of straight, white teeth. "A vodka martini for the gentleman, Maggie my darlin'. And another highball for me." Pusher glanced at Grace. "A glass of tonic water for the little lady."

"Sure thing, Mr. Davis." Maggie picked up Pusher's glass and set it on her tray. "The bar is really crowded tonight so I might be a few extra minutes."

"No problem, honey," Pusher responded with a slow wink. "We're in no hurry."

When Maggie left the table, Grace let impatience get the better of her.

"Since when do you hang out in strip bars?" She glanced pointedly beyond their table to the row of steel poles set on a long narrow stage. Half a dozen woman clad in a rainbow selection of G-strings worked their way around the poles in slow, seductive twirls and slides.

"I don't usually, but under the circumstances..." Pusher shrugged. "A few years back, I did the owner a few favors. That's why I asked you to meet me here. We're practically among friends. Besides, it's easier to keep my ear to the streets here. Fish out information on what happened to Helene."

"Did you find out anything?" Jacob asked.

"Word has it that Helene had hooked up with a major player in the city. Someone who foots big parties for even bigger clients."

"Who?" Jacob snapped out the question before Grace could.

"At this point, it can be anyone. But whoever it is has their fingers in every underground business in this district. Drugs, prostitutes, gambling. You name a sin, they've got the market cornered."

"Do you have Helene's computer?"

"Yes," he said. "I grabbed it before the police arrived. Trouble is, I've accessed most of the files and come up with nothing that might give us a clue why she was murdered."

"Did you bring it?"

"Under the table." Pusher took the stirrer from his glass and tossed it onto a nearby napkin.

"We need that computer, Pusher," Jacob said. "Whoever killed Helene might be after what's in her files."

"You can take it with you. I made a copy of

the files to play with them a little more, just in case there is something encoded."

"What did you find on the computer?" Grace asked.

"That's the interesting part. Other than regular business files for the bar, like accounts and supplies, I discovered a couple of dozen dossiers on some pretty important people."

"Such as?" Jacob leaned forward.

"Articles and notes on the upcoming presidential election. The candidates, the voting, their supporters. A complete workup on Richard D'Agostini. From his college days."

"The Maryland senator?" Grace asked, puzzled.

"The one and the same." Pusher paused. "But he's much more than that. He's the Senate Majority Leader and a pretty powerful force on Capitol Hill."

"Here ya go folks," Maggie stepped up to

the table and placed their drinks in front of them. "If you need anything else, just wave me down. Otherwise I'll check back with you in a little while."

"Thanks darlin'," Pusher said, then waited until Maggie left once again.

"If you were looking for Helene's major player, D'Agostini would be the one at the top of the list," Jacob commented.

"Sure would be." Pusher studied Grace for a second.

"What is it?"

"There was also a file on Alfred Langdon."

"Who is Langdon?" Jacob asked.

"He's the man my mother worked for." Grace frowned. "She was his top aide. He was running for reelection to the Senate. They died together in a plane crash right before the election that year. D'Agostini ran in Langdon's place and won the Senate seat."

"There's a coincidence."

"If you believe in them," Pusher acknowledged. "I don't."

"But why would Helene have that information?"

"She had more than that. She had a complete file on you, Grace."

"Me? Why?"

"Maybe she investigated you before she decided to become partners with you," Pusher commented. "She also had an extensive file on both your parents."

"Did she have anything on me?" Jacob asked.

"Some contact information. Phone numbers. Addresses," Pusher observed. "Didn't realize you were worth so much in worldwide real estate, Lomax. Otherwise I might have been nicer to you."

Jacob raised an eyebrow at that.

Pusher drained his drink. "It's all here." He

reached under the table, pulled out the small laptop bag.

"All of it?" Jacob repeated, his tone sharp.

"I don't double-cross friends, Lomax," Pusher said, his own tone showing the same edge. "Not that you're my friend, but Grace is. I owe her my life. I don't pay my debts with betrayal."

Jacob studied him for a moment, then gave a quick nod.

"The file you want is listed under Primoris."

"Primoris?" Jacob frowned. "That's Latin for first or foremost. So the only good lead we have may be in one of those files."

"How did you figure out the password, Pusher?" Grace asked.

The bar manager shrugged. "I didn't. I bypassed the security and deciphered it afterward."

"You think one of those files will tell us who is behind this?" Grace asked.

"It didn't help me get any closer," Pusher responded. "But it's all we have at the moment. How are you two set for money and transportation?"

"We're fine for now. We're staying—"

"Out of sight," Jacob finished for Grace.

Pusher nodded, understanding.

"One other thing, Pusher. I need to go shopping for some equipment. Hi-tech stuff. Know anyone who doesn't ask questions?"

"Sure." Pusher pulled out a pen from his pocket and wrote an address on the napkin. "The dude who runs this place can hook you up. His name is on the napkin. Just tell him I sent you."

He handed Jacob the information. "If I get more information, where do you want me to contact you?"

"We'll contact you," Jacob said easily enough, then pocketed the napkin. "Soon."

Grace leaned down and kissed the bar manager's cheek. "Thanks, Pusher."

He caught her arm when she was about to turn away. "Be careful, darlin'."

"She will." Jacob cupped her elbow as they made their way through the tables. Suddenly Jacob stopped and swore. "We've got company.

A head above the crowd, it was easy to spot Frank Sweeney. Just then, the enforcer turned. His eyes caught Grace's and she gasped.

"Let's go!" Jacob yelled.

He snagged her hand and pulled. They shoved their way through the crowd, making little headway.

"They're coming." A quick glance told her Sweeney would catch them if she didn't think of something. She reached into her purse, grabbed a handful of cash and threw it up in the air behind them. A wall of people screamed. Strippers, bartenders, customers rushed the floor, diving for the money.

"Of all the—" Jacob swore. "I didn't give you half of our cash, so you could toss it away."

Quickly, they burst through the front doors, then ducked down the side street where they'd left the truck.

"It worked, didn't it?" Grace demanded, when they reached the truck. She automatically stepped to the driver's side. They were broke but safe. That's all Grace cared about.

"I'll drive." Jacob said, his voice barely containing the anger.

"What's the matter?"

"I'd like to know how Sweeney knew we'd be at Chancellor's."

"You don't think Pusher—"

"I won't if you can give me a better explanation."

Grace didn't say anything, simply because she couldn't.

Chapter Fourteen

Pusher threw money on the table and headed out the back. Since he didn't see Jacob and Grace in the throng of people, he'd just have to trust the man could take care of Grace.

He opened the door to the women's dressing room. A few of the girls screamed—mostly the half-naked ones—while others threw clothes and shoes.

"Sorry, ladies," Pusher said with a smile, dodging them and their sailing shoes. Quickly, he made his way to the back exit and stepped out into the alley behind the club.

He took a deep breath, clearing his head of the smoke and stale air. A slight shift in the shadows had him taking a step back and reaching for the pistol in his suit pocket.

"You look like a man with a problem, Pusher." Maggie, cigarette in her hand, stepped into the rim of light.

"Maggie, darlin'." Pusher let his hand fall back to his side. "You scared the hell out of me." He nodded toward the cigarette. "I thought you told me you'd quit those a few weeks ago."

She dropped the butt and smashed it under her heel. "I did, but today…" Maggie stopped. "Never mind."

Pusher liked Maggie. She'd pulled herself up from the gutter. Word had it that she had battled a drug problem for over a year and won. "Look, Magpie, I wish I could hang tonight. But I have important business to take care of. I'll catch you later, okay?"

"Sure, Pusher. I'll see you later."

He straightened his tie and stepped past her. Suddenly a hand gripped his shoulder from behind. Pain shot from his neck to his head. His knees buckled.

"Going somewhere, Pusher?"

The hand turned Pusher just far enough so he could see a man's face.

"Do I know you?"

"The name is Sweeney." The big man looked at his associate. "Pay the lady, Miller."

The second guy took a couple of hundred-dollar bills from his wallet. A big, bullish man with droopy lips and heavy eyelids, Miller wouldn't win any beauty contests, Pusher thought wryly.

"Sorry, Pusher." Maggie stuck the bills into her bra, her eyes meeting his with a quiet defiance even as they filled with tears. "I needed the money." With a sad smile, she turned back down the alley.

"I don't suppose we can talk about this, gents," he said, trying to ignore the death grip on his shoulder.

"Oh, you'll be talking. But to a man named Kragen," Sweeney commented. "He wants discuss a few things with you regarding Grace Renne and her new friend. I suggest you give the right answers, because your life will—" the smaller man grunted in pain as Sweeney squeezed his collarbone to emphasize his point "—depend on it."

"I guess I can spare a few minutes of my time." Pusher's struggle for nonchalance was lost in a painful rasp.

"Glad to hear it. Now I'd rather you walk to our car on your own two feet, but if you, say, get the urge to run, I have no problem throwing you in the car in a few broken pieces. Your choice."

Pusher didn't fight his way from the streets without learning a thing or two about survival.

"If I say okay, can I have my shoulder back?"

Sweeney let go and Pusher hit the ground. Pain exploded through his kneecaps, but he didn't cry out. He rolled his shoulder, helping the blood flow back into his muscles. "I'll have a chat with Kragen. But I'm not quite sure how I can help him."

"By having answers, Pusher. Because if you don't, I can guarantee you won't be able to help yourself."

"Lead the way, gentlemen," Pusher joked before he stood and dusted off his suit.

Sweeney shoved him forward. "You first."

Chapter Fifteen

The impound lot was located on the outskirts of town and hard to miss. As far as Grace knew, it was the only ten-foot-high chain-link fence topped with spirals of barbed wire in a fifty-mile radius of Annapolis.

"There's a good chance the perimeter is wired," Jacob muttered. He glanced down at his arm. "I'm going to cut through the fence. Which means I'm going to need your help."

Grace raised an eyebrow, wondering how much it cost him to make that confession.

"Shouldn't we wait until midnight? Ten o'clock seems a little early."

"They shut down at six. The security guard is the only one we have to worry about." He handed her his Glock. "Ever shot a gun?"

"No." The steel was warm and smooth against her palm, surprising her. She expected the steel to be cold, the grip rough.

"Keep an eye out for the security guards. And for God's sake, don't shoot them."

"Then why give me a gun?"

"Because our friends might be out there, too. If you see one of them, aim for their chest and empty the clip."

He grabbed a small laser cutter from the backpack at his feet. "I'm going to keep the cuts low, so both my hands are going to be busy."

"I'll keep watch." Grace scanned the yard. More than a hundred parked cars lined the lot under the yellow glow of flood lights. It was like looking for the proverbial needle in a haystack.

As if he knew what she was thinking, Jacob said, "You're wasting your time. We don't need the car, we need the keys."

He nodded toward the trailer office to the left of their position. "I'm betting the keys are hanging in there."

The chain-link fencing broke free. Just as he lifted the bottom edge to slide under, dogs barked in the distance. "Figures. Cops' budget. Cheaper security and no pension plans."

Jacob cursed, then glanced at the gun.

Understanding, Grace whispered. "I'm not shooting the guard dogs."

He shrugged, letting the fence fall back into place. "Just a thought."

"Find another."

Suddenly, two German shepherds hit the fence at a dead run, their barks shattering the night air.

"How fast can you run?"

Grace watched the animals growl, their teeth bared back to their molars. "Not funny."

Jacob sat back on his heels. "Okay, let's go with plan B."

"What's plan B?"

"Back to the car."

Grace followed him to the truck and slid into the passenger seat. "We're just going to leave?"

He glanced at her. "Buckle up." Then he twisted wires together, starting the ignition. With suppressed annoyance, he shoved the truck into Reverse. "Hold on to something," he ordered, then punched the gas.

Too late, Grace realized his intention. The truck plowed through the locked gate of the lot.

"Are you crazy?" She screamed and grabbed for the dashboard.

He whipped the truck around and aimed for

the wooden porch in front of the portable office trailer.

Within seconds, they plowed through, smashing the wood and scraping the side panel with a loud screech.

"Roll down your window and get ready to get us the hell out of here."

Within seconds, he crawled over her and climbed out the window and up on the roof of the truck's cab.

The dogs hit the truck, their teeth bared, their bodies trembling with anger as they jumped up against the driver's window.

Jacob kicked the trailer door in on the second try and slid from the roof in through the office doorway.

Immediately, Grace slid over to the driver's seat. "Come on," she murmured and gripped the wheel. In the distance, she could hear a set of sirens, certain they were heading in their direction.

A few minutes later, Jacob tossed a garbage bag full of keys in through the passenger window before climbing through himself.

"Go!"

Grace hit the gas and sped out of the parking lot, relieved when both dogs stopped their chase a block away from the impound.

She glanced over at Jacob. "Your shoulder is bleeding."

"I probably ripped open the stitches." He leaned his head against the back of the seat and closed his eyes. The wind washed over him, cooling the damp sweat on his skin. "But no dogs were hurt."

She nodded toward the bag. "You didn't know which keys were mine."

"Nope. So I grabbed them all."

"They'll know now that I helped you. There were cameras."

"Grace, there are always cameras."

In his mind's eye, he saw the flash. Helene was laughing at him—her face masked, her body sheethed in black spandex climbing gear. They were suspended from the side of building, hanging on ropes with pulleys.

Be careful, we've got cameras at two o'clock.

Darling, Helene laughed softly, there are always cameras.

The image faded into a frustrating void. He waited for more of the memory to break free. But no more came.

Earlier, when they left the house, Grace followed the truck with the SUV. "Time to ditch the truck. The front headlight is out, so be careful. We can't risk getting pulled over before we get it out of the way."

They left the truck parked on a deserted

street and walked to Jacob's SUV two blocks away. "Do you have a key chain for your keys so I can find them easier?"

"It's a USB thumb drive in a black leather key chain." Grace stopped. "Do you think it would be that simple? She could've switched my USB with one of hers at the restaurant yesterday. I wouldn't have noticed."

"If she did, it won't be simple. Those keys sat at the bottom of the bay for a good three hours or more."

Once in the SUV, Grace drove while Jacob searched for her keys. It took a good fifteen minutes before he finally located them. "The leather case protected it to some extent but it's still wet."

"Does that mean it's ruined?"

"Possibly." He examined the small thumb drive. "But a USB memory stick has no moving parts and we're at the north end of the bay. With all the rains, that part of the bay is likely more fresh water than salt water right now. We could get lucky."

"We need a blow-dryer," Grace suggested.

"Blow-dryer might damage it. Our best bet is to let it dry naturally," Jacob reasoned. "But we might not have the time."

"Could the password code from my phone be for the files?"

"Hell, we don't even know if this holds the missing files. For all we know, it could be Helene's grocery list."

"I CAN APPRECIATE a man who wants to deal, Pusher." Oliver Kragen leaned against the bar in the gymnasium. "But some things I just don't haggle over."

Earlier, he ordered Sweeney to handcuff the bar manager to a chair. Not because he expected the younger man to escape but simply to keep him in the chair once the inter-rogation started taking its toll.

Which, in all honesty, the bar manager passed a good hour before the toll showed.

Pusher's head dropped forward against his chest. Blood dripped from the broken nose and split lips, soaking the shirt beneath.

Kragen nodded to Sweeney, who placed a bottle of ammonia under Pusher's nose to bring him around.

"Pusher, we need to establish some kind of rapport here." He grabbed the younger man's hair and forced his head back until he was looking straight up into Oliver's eyes.

Pusher's face was no more than blood and ripped skin. Not surprising to Oliver, consid-ering skin never held up well against leather-covered fists.

"Now, I'm going to ask you again where Helene Garrett's computer is."

"I told you Lomax has it," Pusher answered, his words slurred by his swollen lips.

"But you failed to tell me where Lomax is."

"I don't know. They were to get in touch with me."

"About what?"

"Updates on Helene's murder."

"And this disk I found in your pocket?" When Pusher's head lolled forward, Oliver slapped it back. "The disk!"

"I don't know. Haven't had a chance to look at it yet."

That earned Pusher another backhand across the face. Oliver nodded to Sweeney, who walked over to a nearby desk.

He slid the disk into the laptop computer.

"We need a password," said Sweeney after looking at the screen. "I could probably find someone to break it."

"That would take too much time. Besides,"

Oliver reflected, as he glanced down at Pusher, "I have the feeling the answer is right here on the tip of Pusher's tongue. We just need to convince Mr. Davis that giving us the password might just save that same tongue."

"TAKE A LOOK at this, Jacob."

It was after two in the morning, but Grace wasn't willing to go to bed until they read Helene's computer files.

"Oliver Kragen. Top aide to Senator D'Agostini." She rubbed the gritty fatigue from her eyes. Then looked again. "I've seen this guy before."

"With Helene?"

"I don't remember. Maybe at a political event."

"Pusher said she had detailed files on a lot of people."

"Including me, my father and mother. From

the time my parents met in the military to my mother's death. And my father after."

"According to this," Jacob said, scrolling down, "your dad had top security clearance."

"What do you mean? He was a spy?"

"Not necessarily. He could have been in charge of a specific project, or even a specific part of the government or war department." Jacob pinched his nose between his forefinger and thumb. Without thinking, he walked to the kitchen cabinet, found the aspirin and took a few.

It wasn't until he finished swallowing the tablets dry that he realized what he'd done. Obviously, on some level he remembered where the pills were located.

"She's got complete files on several of her business acquaintances. And on Pusher and myself, too."

"But?" Jacob glanced at Grace, impatient.

"Pusher was right, she has nothing on you, Jacob." She paused, considering. "Other than a few addresses. Why?"

JACOB HEARD BRANCHES banging against the house. He tensed, and then relaxed. He blinked away the grit in his eyes and slowly flexed the stiffness from his bad shoulder.

He glanced over at Grace, gave in to the urge to smooth away the stray strand of hair on her cheek. Why had he walked away from her? She shifted closer, partially lying on him.

It took him a while to convince her to share the bed with him. But he did so on the pretense he didn't want to mistake her for an intruder.

She accepted his suggestion only after he agreed to sleep on top of the blankets. But in the end, it didn't matter. She moved restlessly in her sleep and kicked off her covers.

His hand automatically came up, drifted

over her spine. She'd changed her clothes, finding a pair of black jogging pants to use for pajamas and a thin cotton T-shirt as her top.

The hem had worked its way up past her waist. Unable to stop himself, he placed his hand over her belly, just above her panty line. The pregnancy had hardened her stomach. Something in him shifted. Something he didn't look at too closely. Not yet.

He noticed a tattoo just inside the curve of her hip. His fingers slid over the delicate tracings of the butterfly wings.

Why a butterfly?

She smiled, running a hand up over his hip. Why the scar?

The memory stopped him. It wasn't the first. He'd been having bits and pieces all night since the one of Helene.

But the few he had after were all of Grace.

Her on a lounger beside a pool. Both of

them sailing the bay. Romantic dinners. Evenings at the theater. Even more evenings at her home in front of the fire.

Each memory connected. Each ending with them kissing or making love.

But when? Five months ago? A year? He didn't know. Winter. Aspen. Long enough to have fathered the baby? He'd suspected all along, but suspecting and having proof were two different things.

Restless, he snagged a pair of jeans by the bed, slipped them up over his hips, only to pause before zipping.

It was there, just at the top point of his right hip. A jagged, raised mark six inches in length.

Why the scar? she'd asked.

Frustrated that he had no answer, he grabbed the phone off of the nightstand, then slowly climbed the stairs to the tower.

Once up at the top, he tried Pusher's

number. But after letting it ring several times, he hung up.

Where in the hell was he?

He heard it then, the soft pad of her feet against the wood steps. "I didn't mean to wake you."

She sighed. "The baby decided to sleep on my bladder. But since you'd been gone so long, I wanted to make sure you were okay. What time is it?"

"After five in the morning," he said and sat on one of the window seats. He forced himself to look at her, study the delicate lines of her face, the soft waves of blond hair that settled on her shoulders. Beautiful, rumpled and decidedly feminine. Something moved inside him. The queer mixture of fear and vulnerability that came with the sense of inevitability. "You should go to bed, Grace. You need rest. If not for you, for the baby."

"The baby is fine," she murmured and

stepped closer. He caught a new scent, the spicy scent of his soap she'd used earlier. A fist of desire tightened his gut, caused him to shift away.

Annoyed at his retreat, Jacob pushed the phone into his front pocket, drawing her attention.

"No answer still?"

"None. I think something happened to him."

"Something bad?"

"Something. I don't know what. He could have skipped town. Got thrown in jail again. Defected to the other side."

"I won't believe that. Not Pusher."

"Well, we aren't doing anything about it until tomorrow." Jacob looked out the window at predawn sky. "We'll start with the strip club and work our way from there," he said, then rubbed the back of his neck. "Look, Grace, I don't want you hurt—"

"Then I guess we better figure this all out soon," she responded softly. "Okay?"

The set of his jaw told her it wasn't okay. "Since we're both up anyway, let's see if we can prod your memory," she suggested, trying to distract him with a change of subject. Giving in to impulse, she brushed a stray lock of hair from his forehead.

"Tell me something I didn't know before when we were together," he insisted. He caught her hand, tugged on it until she sat in his lap.

"I was named after a prayer."

"Which one?"

"The Serenity Prayer," she said, her words lost against his neck as she rested her head against his good shoulder. She missed this, the closeness.

As if sensing her thoughts, his arms tightened around her, keeping her safe if only for that moment. "What were the words?" He whispered the question against her hair, making her smile.

"'God, give me grace to accept with serenity the things that cannot be changed, courage to change the things which should be changed, and the wisdom to understand the difference.'"

"Who wrote it?"

"No one knows for sure." After a moment, she added, "It was my mother's favorite, though."

"God, give me Grace," he repeated. She could feel his smile against her ear. "Honey, it's probably a good thing you're mother didn't name you Serenity."

Grace pulled back until her eyes met his. "That's exactly what she used to say." She winked, slow and deliberate. The surge of pleasure rolled through Jacob, catching him off guard. How could he forget a look like that?

"In fact, she swears that when they decided

on my name, the earth trembled, just enough for her to know she was in trouble."

"You miss her, don't you?"

"Very much."

Jacob watched the moonlight halo her head, setting the golden highlights on fire. He gave in to the impulse and captured a few strands in his hand. Just then a second flash of memory hit him. "I kissed you here, before."

"Yes."

"It wasn't a friendly kiss, Grace."

"No, it wasn't."

He leaned in until his mouth hovered just above hers. "Anything you need to tell me?"

"Not if I can help it—"

He covered her mouth with his and breathed in her sigh, keeping the kiss light until a sexy purr rounded off the edge of her breath. It took him from comfort to desire in a millisecond.

What man wouldn't take the kiss deeper to

hear that sound again, feel the roll from her throat to his gut?

His hand twisted in her hair, keeping her head still in case she wanted to pull away. He dove this time, swallowing her in one, long erotic gulp of sin and sex.

But Grace couldn't pull away. She couldn't think. She couldn't breathe. All she could do was leave herself open under the onslaught. Matching him stroke for stroke, taste for taste, texture upon delicious texture.

When that wasn't enough, when it didn't come close to enough, he brought her up against him, his body hard as much as hers was pliant. When her knees threatened to knock, she thought for a moment of sliding off his lap, giving herself some space, regaining some sanity.

But then he dove again and she managed not to think at all.

Jacob's hand cupped her thigh, keeping her in place. But she had no thought of moving. He squeezed gently, kneading the flesh beneath his fingers, letting his thumb stray in long lazy circles, tempting her to shift and then, moments later, to move against him when he upped the tempo.

When she trembled, Jacob slipped his hand over her belly, groaning when it quivered beneath his fingers.

He nuzzled her neck, followed the cord of it to her collarbone, suckled her nipple through the cotton of her tee. The tremors ripped through her as his fingers slid between her thighs, stroking her until her hips writhed, her muscles quivered.

"Let it go, let me see."

The warm, moist demand against her ear sent her over the edge. Grace erupted, clenching herself around his hand, riding the release, melting into him as it played out.

"I can't believe I've forgotten that," he whispered the words against her neck. Visibly affected, he kissed her, soothed her trembling body with long, draining kisses until she quieted beneath his touch.

"You're shaking," Grace whispered against his chest. "You're whole body… you've never—"

He raised her chin with his hand, ignoring the slight tremor in his fingers. "Maybe you are finally seeing the real me. Maybe we both are. With no memories, I have nothing to guard against."

The truth of his statement hit her square in the chest. "A relationship with you is impossible, Jacob. You're still the same man. When all is said and done, those guards will go back up once the amnesia is gone." She softened the harsh words by kissing his neck. "You didn't want me then. What good would it do to become lovers again, after all this time?"

"Damn it, we never stopped being lovers, Grace."

"Yes, we did. The minute you walked away from us."

He stilled. "Us?"

"You and me," she snapped, using her finger to point back and forth between them.

For a moment, he'd thought she meant her and the baby. That he'd left her and the baby. "I really did a number on you, didn't I?"

Her silence gave him her answer.

"I'm sorry, honey. I think if I could take it back—" he murmured, then stiffened.

"What?"

"Shh." He instinctively placed his hand over her mouth. Then he heard it again. A car door shutting.

"We've got company." He looked out the

tower window and saw two sedans parked outside. "Sweeney."

Grace tensed. "But how?"

"Ask Pusher," Jacob said grimly. "In fact, I'll ask him the next time I see him."

A trunk slammed shut. "They're not worried about surprising us."

"Why?"

"Probably because of all the guns their carrying."

Chapter Sixteen

Hugh Miller was the first to speak up. "Are they there?"

"Don't see them, but Lomax would be smarter than that," Sweeney answered, looking through infrared binoculars. "If I were a betting man, I'd say the odds are in our favor. This was the closest address of Lomax's on the list."

Sweeney took his pistol from his side holster. "If they are there, I want them taken alive. Got that?" Sweeney waved the other three men over. Miller checked his clip. "We need them breathing. Anyone who kills them by accident will be dead before Lomax or Renne hits the ground. Understand me?"

The other men nodded.

"Then let's go."

"GRAB YOUR JACKET and shoes! Now!"

They raced down the tower's stairs to the bedroom beneath. "The car?"

"No. It's too late for that. We're going to have to go across the bay."

Grace followed him down to the lowest level, her own sneakers in hand.

"Get down in the boat."

Within moments, she lay flat on her belly, curled at the bottom.

"No matter what, I don't want you sitting up." Jacob grabbed a nearby gas container and started pouring it over the dock.

The fumes caught in her throat, making her gag. "What are you doing?"

"Making sure they can't follow us."

He jumped into the boat and untied the rope from the post. It wasn't until then he noticed the anchor had been set overboard.

Quickly, he pulled it to the surface.

He swore. Grace glanced over and in the darkness she could see a large bag tied to the anchor weight.

Jacob tossed it into the boat. "What do you want to bet I've found my stash."

He left it and grabbed a life jacket. "Put this on." He took a lighter from his pocket, hit the switch and tossed it onto the dock. Flames immediately spread. "Hold your shirt over your nose."

"Your house, Jacob. You're burning—"

"If I'm as rich as you say, I'll have it rebuilt later."

He slammed the accelerator forward. Gunfire peppered their boat as Sweeney's men shot out from the dock, but none of the bullets hit close.

Grace peered over the side, saw headlights turned on in the distance. "They're following us," Grace yelled the words across the din of the motor.

"It will be hard to follow us without a boat." Jacob studied a bank of trees crowding the beach in the distance. He brought the boat around until it pointed directly toward woods rising over the crest of land.

"Hold on." He jerked the steering wheel until the boat headed straight for the beach. "This is going to get rough."

Chapter Seventeen

In the daylight the Chancellor's was nothing more than drab. Drab brown paint, drab gray cement. Even the neon light, blinking in the afternoon sun, lost the power to catch and hold the gaze of the few pedestrians who strolled past.

Jacob and Grace arrived at the strip club before its doors opened for the nooners escaping their jobs for a lunch hour of distraction and drinks.

"There she is," Jacob murmured, his gaze

settling on the street about half a block down from their rented silver sedan.

It took over two hours to find a stretch of beach to ditch the boat, steal another car and head back into the city. And then another hour or so to secure the rented car and check Pusher's apartment.

"Let's go." They had been leaning against the car, waiting. Jacob cupped her elbow and guided her across the street until they intersected with Maggie at the alleyway entrance beside the club.

The blonde tossed her cigarette into the gutter just as they approached. Half expecting her to bolt, Grace braced herself, blocking the waitress's path.

"Hi, Maggie, do you remember us?" Jacob asked.

"Sure, you're Pusher's friends."

She folded her arms across her stomach.

But it was her bloodshot eyes that drew Grace's attention.

"Actually, we're looking for Pusher and wondered if you'd seen him."

The waitress looked at Jacob. "You a cop?"

"No."

"You've got the smell of a cop."

"Pusher's my friend, Maggie," Grace said quietly.

"Well, hoorah for you."

"Last night, I got the impression Pusher was your friend, too," Grace added mildly.

"Then you got the wrong impression." Maggie tried to step past but Jacob grabbed her arm and held her in place.

"Let me go." She jerked her arm away, but Jacob gripped tighter. "I'll call a cop."

"You do that, Maggie, and you'll lose out. I'm willing to pay for information."

"How much?"

"Two hundred."

"Make it five and you have a deal."

"Okay, five."

Her eyes narrowed with suspicion. "Show me."

Jacob pulled out his wallet and took out five one-hundred-dollar bills. "They're yours if I get the answers I want."

Maggie stared at the money for a moment. "Okay. That guy who chased you last night? His name is Sweeney."

"We already know that."

"Well, what you don't know is that Sweeney and his goons went after Pusher a few minutes after you left," she said. "Yesterday, one of Sweeney's guys put the word on the street that he wanted to talk to Pusher. He left his card at all of Pusher's haunts. Rumor was that Sweeney was looking for something Pusher had. Said he'd pay good money to just talk to Pusher."

"So when Pusher showed up here yesterday—"

"I called Sweeney. I told him you two were with Pusher and Sweeney went ballistic on the phone, ya know? He started cussing a blue streak. I thought he was going to hang up but then he told me if I saw you start to leave before he arrived, I was to stall you if I could."

"Why didn't you?"

"Before I could think of something," she said, then nodded at Grace, "your girlfriend threw all the money on the floor." She shrugged. "I stopped and grabbed a few twenties myself since I couldn't reach you anyway."

"You still haven't told me what Sweeney did with Pusher."

"Give me half first."

"Two hundred," Jacob said and handed over two of the bills. She stuck them in her bra.

"Sweeney cornered Pusher in the alley last

night. He forced Pusher to go with him. Sweeney said some guy named Kragen wanted to have a talk with Pusher." She glanced up the street. "I don't know what about. I'd already gotten my money so I left."

"Did you say Kragen? As in Oliver Kragen?"

"I don't know. I just heard the last name."

Jacob took the last three bills and stuffed them into her bra himself. "Thanks. I'll make sure I pass along your story to Pusher when I see him."

"You do that." Maggie tossed over her shoulder as she walked toward the club. "If you need anything else, sugar," she added, deliberately adopting Pusher's accent, "you all don't forget to look me up."

For the first time, Grace noted Jacob's hands fisted in anger. "We need to find Pusher," he said. "I'm pretty sure I'm the type that would rather give an apology in person."

"Where do you think Sweeney took him?"

"I don't know, but I do know who does."

"Kragen," Grace stated.

"How would you like to attend a presidential election ball tonight?"

"I think I'd love to."

Chapter Eighteen

The Lakelear Grand Hotel stood on posh Connecticut Avenue. Labeled as more of a resort than hotel, Grace had to admit she'd never had the budget for a suite.

She glanced over at Jacob as he pulled up to the front entrance. "How much money was in that bag?" They had already used a good chunk, she thought, to shop for clothes, suitcases and other necessities.

"Enough not to worry about staying here for a while."

The valet opened the door. They had traded the sedan in earlier for a black Porsche. Grace swung her legs out, deliberately waiting to catch the valet's eye before stepping out of the rented Porsche.

"Welcome to the Lakelear."

"Thank you," she said, smoothing her carmel suede midthigh skirt back into place.

His smile slowly disappeared as Jacob rounded the hood of the Porsche. "Welcome to Lakelear Grand, sir."

Jacob just nodded, having already given his key to another valet. He cupped Grace's elbow. "Ready, darling?"

"Yes."

The hotel lobby lived up to the glamour and wealth of the D.C. elite, with its marble inlay floor and gold-trimmed reception desk.

"Welcome, sir. May I help you?" A man

stood behind the cherrywood counter. His small mustache twitched only slightly.

"My name is John Eckert. My secretary made arrangements for a suite earlier today."

"Yes, Mr. Eckert we've been waiting for you. My name is William Fremont and I'm the assistant manager here at the Lakelear. All your arrangements have been taken care of." He nodded to include Grace, hesitating a long second.

Jacob pointedly ignored the silent request for an introduction. He didn't want to take any chances that her voice would be recognized as his secretary's.

The assistant manager shifted his gaze just over Grace's shoulder. "George will be happy to escort you to your suite." He handed the card to a young man in a bellboy uniform. "The Mayflower Suite, George."

"Follow me, sir."

"One moment." Jacob turned back to the assistant manager.

"Yes, sir."

"It seems one of our pieces of luggage has been forgotten and we'll need replacement clothes for our evening plans. I'll need to be measured for a tuxedo and have several gowns delivered to our room from your clothing boutiques. Have them call our room for the details."

"My pleasure, Mr. Eckert."

Jacob placed his hand at the small of Grace's back as they followed the bellboy.

"Room service work for you?"

It had already been a long afternoon. The boutique had sent up a selection of gowns and the men's shop had sent up their tailor. Both Jacob and Grace were ready for their appearance later that night.

"Maybe a vanilla shake, if you don't mind. My stomach is a little queasy," Grace added, thinking about Pusher. "The shake will help settle it."

As if reading her thoughts, Jacob walked over to her and pulled her to him, wrapping his arms around her. "No, I don't mind but I'm going to order some fruit and a sandwich with it. Try to eat what you can. Pusher will be fine. They won't do anything to him, for a while at least. They want what's on the USB thumb drive. Until they get it, they can't be sure what part he plays in this."

Grace knew Jacob was exaggerating, but there was an underlying truth to his words.

"I'm also worried that someone might recognize you," Grace reasoned. "Unlike me, you wouldn't have any idea who your friends or your enemies are at the ball."

"From what you've said, I don't have too

many friends to worry about. That should narrow the playing field."

"That's not funny."

He sighed and placed his forehead against hers. "No, its not. And neither is this situation," he said apologetically. "Look, I've had time to think about the amnesia, Grace. There's nothing I can do about getting my memories back, so I'll just have to learn to punt. Seems that's second nature to me anyway."

"I can't disagree with that."

His hand cupped her jaw, then lifted her face up until she met his gaze. "But I don't think it's second nature to you. That's why I don't want you with me. It's too dangerous. For you and the baby."

"We're going to a swank ball at the Senate Majority Leader's mansion, not a drug dealer's lair."

"Bad guys don't have a dress code."

"I'll be fine," she said. "If there's trouble, I'll lose myself in the crowd like we agreed. Then leave after you've caused a diversion."

"I'll have to accept that, for now," Jacob said. "Why don't you go have a shower? The food will be here by the time you get out. Then after you eat, you can try and get some rest. It's going to be a long night."

"A shower sounds good." But they both noted she didn't comment on the rest of Jacob's statement.

"Most of this kind of work is a waiting game, Grace. We've got hours before the ball."

"What kind of work?"

"Government work," Jacob said automatically, then froze. He tried to follow that same train of thought, only to draw another blank. "Damn it."

"It's a start, Jacob," she said softly and kissed his cheek. "If you worked as an agent, you'd have to keep that from me, wouldn't you?"

"More than likely," he admitted. "But I wouldn't let me off the hook that easily, Grace. For all we know, I could be one of the bad guys."

"No way," she quipped, walking toward the bath. "You dress too nice."

His laughter followed her into the bathroom, making her smile. The old Jacob rarely laughed. So whenever she managed to get him chuckling, she counted it as a victory.

She stripped out of her clothes. On impulse, she studied her image in the mirror. Her breasts had gotten larger, the nipples much darker. A small hard bulge in her tummy told her the baby was growing. The small flutters she'd been feeling on and off told her he was getting more active. For precautionary reasons, she checked for spotting before folding her clothes and placing them on the vanity nearby.

It was hard for her to believe that less than forty hours earlier, she'd been in her house, taking it easy and baking cookies.

Alone.

Chapter Nineteen

On the Hill, there was a saying: Good politics require great staging.

Which made Senator D'Agostini's presidential campaign ball a full-blown Hollywood extravaganza.

Palladian windows were draped in patriotic blue, while diamond-infused chandeliers glittered and sparkled from twenty-foot coffered ceilings.

A sea of satin, silk and tailored tuxedos crowded thirty square yards of glossy herringbone wood, while a fifty-piece orchestra stood in the corner delivering a jaunty but sophisticated big-band sound.

"Dance with me."

Before Grace could react, Jacob's fingers skimmed over the small of her back, urging her forward into the crush of waltzing couples.

They made a striking pair. Jacob had opted for a basic black tuxedo. Severe in cut, the sleek but simple material complemented his broad shoulders, his lean hips. The arrogance of the cut went well with his predatory gaze, the dangerous slant of his chiseled features. A panther, she thought, stalking his prey.

He pulled her to him, holding her in the close intimate circle of his arms. Making it apparent to anyone watching that they didn't want to be disturbed.

He bent his head close to hers. "Relax," he murmured.

"I am," she whispered back, hoping that saying the words out loud would make them true. Gaining access had been relatively simple. All one needed was to mingle, to laugh and part with a compliment or two about one's golf game or latest insider news on Wall Street. "My role is easy. I'm just the arm candy."

And for that purpose, she'd chosen a strapless gown of ivory silk chiffon. Feminine and alluring, the overlay material flowed from a bodice that hugged her breasts before falling gracefully into a cascaded drape of shirred layers.

She pinned her hair up high on her head, drawing more than one male gaze to the slope of her neck. And more than one female's glance to the diamond solitaires that winked at her earlobes.

"God, you're beautiful." His fingers drifted carelessly over the delicate point of her shoulder, sending ripples of pleasure down her spine.

His arm pressed her closer, until the heat of him seeped through the thin layers of her gown. Grace got lost in the sway of their bodies. She breathed in his warm, masculine scent. Caught the underlying hint of after-shave. She rested her head on his shoulder, promising herself only one song.

Suddenly, he went rigid against her. Her gaze snapped to his. The blue of his irises glittered with a fierceness, a cold savage fury that she'd never seen before. An air of violence suddenly surrounded them both like a tight leash.

A small flutter of panic worked its way up at the back of her throat. "Jacob?"

JACOB HEARD HIS NAME, the plea in Grace's voice through the static of sounds, the rush of images.

Suddenly, he was in an alley. It was dark. Pitch-black, he remembered. Glass crackled beneath his feet—the remnants of the alley's light, shattered by a bullet.

Gunfire spattered the Dumpster above Helene's head. *Get behind me.* But the warning came too late.

Pain exploded in his shoulder, but it was Helene who'd screamed, Helene who'd fallen. Frantic, Jacob reached for her, firing his pistol as he pulled her into his lap.

Blood covered her chest, rattled her lungs. *"Jacob...find Grace."*

The grief welled up inside, then seeped through his pores.

He grabbed her tight, willing her to live.

"Jacob. You're hurting me."

Relief poured through him. He blinked, refocusing.

"Jacob," Grace whispered, her voice harsh with worry or fear, he couldn't be sure.

"Grace." He glanced around the dance floor, satisfied no one really cared that they'd stopped dancing.

He automatically took up the rhythm of music. "Are you okay?"

"Yes. Just had a flashback, but I'm fine now." He shifted, forcing the muscles in his back to relax.

"Kragen's here."

"Where?" The muscles snapped into tight rubber bands.

"Over your left shoulder."

He maneuvered her around in a slow, lazy circle. Oliver stopped across the room in front of an older gentleman. Jacob recognized the tall, thin, almost frail build. The gray ring of hair that circled a nearly bald head. "D'Agostini," Jacob commented.

Oliver leaned in to the senator, whispered something by the older man's ear, then stepped back again. The senator nodded. Within moments, the senator excused himself from the ball.

"Where are they going?"

"I don't know but we need to find out," Jacob said, realizing the need for revenge had been forgotten—until now. "He's our only lead to Pusher."

Jacob cupped Grace's elbow and led her off the floor.

OLIVER KRAGEN wasn't happy. There was nothing left to get out of Pusher Davis. The man had taken a beating without uttering one word of information. But for some reason, the senator wanted him kept alive.

"Going somewhere, Kragen?" Before Oliver could react, his arm was shoved up and behind his shoulder. Pain rushed up his back and exploded into his rotator cuff.

It would take very little pressure for Lomax to separate his shoulder. He felt a gun jab in his side. "How the hell did you get in here?"

"Doesn't seem your security is worth the money you pay," Jacob answered. He did a quick search of Kragen's pockets. "Although I have to say that you dress them well.

"Now unless you want to get intimately acquainted with a dialysis machine for the rest of your life, I suggest you do as I ask."

"And that is?" Oliver asked.

"Pusher Davis."

"Who?"

Kragen hissed with pain as Jacob applied pressure to his arm, moving it farther up his back. "I don't think you want me to snap your shoulder out of joint, do you?"

"Okay, say he is here. He's…incapacitated at the moment. You would never be able to get him out without notice."

"You let me worry about that, Oliver. All you need to do is take me to him," Jacob replied, his tone mild. "Agreeably. Pretend we're long lost friends." He punctuated his order with another jab of his pistol.

"And if we're seen?"

"You better hope we're not. Because you'll be the first person I'll want out of the way."

Kragen led them to a room on the third floor. In front stood a man, one of the personal bodyguards Jacob assumed.

He jabbed at Oliver's side.

"It's okay, Miller. These people are associates." The tone of Kragen's voice was smooth but firm.

"Grace."

Grace pulled out a small revolver, aimed it at Miller and fired. A dart imbedded itself in Miller's chest. No more than three seconds later, the giant crumpled to the floor.

Jacob shoved Oliver into the door. The senator's aide punched in the key code with his free hand.

Jacob opened the door. "Go, Grace."

Grace stepped through the door and stopped. Pusher lay unconscious on the bed, his wrists in handcuffs, his face nothing more than raw meat and blood.

Jacob stiffened at Grace's cry of alarm, turned slightly to make sure she was safe.

Without warning, Kragen rammed his elbow into Jacob's gut and twisted away. He grabbed for the gun, but Jacob let go of the grip, catching Oliver off guard. Instead, Jacob nailed the aide in the throat, then slammed his elbow into the man's face. He grunted in satisfaction when he felt the bone give beneath the impact.

Jacob snagged the pistol as Oliver went to his knees. He forced the man's head back by his hair and shoved the barrel under his chin.

Kragen gasped, trying to find his breath through the bruised larynx.

"Jacob. Don't."

Something in Jacob went cold. Grace's plea saved Kragen's life. He slammed the pistol against Oliver's temple and watched him crumple to the floor.

He turned to Grace, took in the fear on her ashen face.

"I didn't kill him."

The savagery of his features told her he could've killed him, would have, if she hadn't been there.

Quickly, Jacob went back to the doorway and dragged Miller into the room. "There's a chance he hadn't been spotted yet by the security cameras."

Grace barely heard. She was already at Pusher's side. "How are we going to get him out of here?" she asked.

Jacob didn't answer. Instead, he handed her the gun and lifted Pusher up and over his good shoulder. His features tightened with the effort, but he didn't waver.

"Let's go. I noticed a service elevator farther down," Jacob said, shifting Pusher slightly. "The only way to do this is make a dash for it."

They headed down the hallway, the thick carpet masking their footsteps. Grace's hand trembled against the gun. Nausea reared up in her stomach, swiped at the back of her throat. But she refused to give in to the queasiness. If they ran into one of D'Agostini's men, she wouldn't hesitate to shoot.

When they reached the elevator, Grace hit the button. Neither of them spoke. With the hall empty, their voices would carry. In the distance they heard a door slam, then muffled footsteps.

Suddenly, the chime sounded and the door

slid open. The voices morphed into screams of rage.

"Go!" Jacob ordered, but Grace was already through the door. Panicked, Grace hit the basement floor first. Then punched the Close button with her fist.

"That won't make it shut any faster."

"I know, but it sure makes me feel better."

"We'll be fine, if we don't have to stop," Jacob said and took the gun from Grace. It wasn't until she looked down, she saw how badly her hands were shaking.

"It's all right, baby. You did good." He raised the gun, barrel up, ready to shoot when the doors slid open once again.

No one was waiting. Relief threatened to buckle her knees.

As if reading her mind, Jacob said, "We're not out of the woods, yet."

Suddenly, gunshots punctuated his statement.

"Move, Grace." They burst through the kitchen doors. Kragen followed less than a minute later. One of the cooks, a small man brandishing a knife, tried to stop them. Jacob laid him out cold with one punch.

"They'll have guards coming at us from both directions," Jacob said as they strode through the maze of ovens and counters. The kitchen staff yelled and cursed until they saw Jacob's gun. Then they screamed.

Suddenly, fire alarms exploded around them. The lights went out. The screams hit a higher pitch as people scrambled for exits.

"Jacob, here," Grace shouted. She stood in front of large garbage chute, holding its steel door open. "It should be big enough."

Quickly, he shoved Pusher down the garbage slide. He picked up Grace and tossed her in, ignoring her scream as she flew down the steel ramp.

Swearing, he dived in after her, a flurry of bullets exploding around him.

"Go!"

Grace jumped out of the Dumpster. Jacob grabbed Pusher and literally threw him into Grace's arms before jumping out himself. Once again, he slung Pusher over his shoulder. With gun in hand, Jacob joined Grace and they headed for the valet parking lot.

People poured from the mansion in a surge of chaos and indignation.

"What's going on?" A young kid, no more than twenty years of age, pulled up in a four-door sedan. His valet badge identified him as Peter. "Is it a fire or something?"

"Why don't you go check it out?" Jacob walked right up to the car and placed the gun in the young man's face. "Now."

"Yes, sir." The guy stumbled out of the car. "I don't want any trouble."

"Then go."

When the kid took off over the lawn, Jacob handed Grace his gun. "You're going to have to drive." He brought Pusher around to the back of the car. With difficulty, he laid the unconscious man in the backseat and then climbed into the passenger seat.

As soon as he was in the car, Grace hit the accelerator and took off through the gate and down the street.

"How are we doing so far?" She blew a stray lock of hair off her forehead.

Jacob checked the side mirror. "We're safe enough for now, but I think it's time to regroup back at the hotel."

"In a stolen car?"

"We'll ditch the car."

She glanced at Pusher through the rearview mirror. "We're going to look petty conspicuous walking into to a hotel like this."

"Who says we need to walk in?"

OLIVER SLAMMED OPEN his office door, nearly taking it off its hinges.

The bruise across his nose had turned purple, but the swelling was down. Oliver held a white kerchief up to the side of his head, stemming the stream of blood still oozing from the cut.

"Who set off the fire alarm?"

Unflustered, Frank Sweeney followed his boss into the office. "Still working on it. But Lomax and the woman got away."

"Of course they did." Kragen slammed his free hand against the desktop. "I want it on the news. Now! If we can't locate them, we'll market them as criminals and hang them out to dry. By tomorrow, I want their faces splashed across every channel in this country. Fugitives wanted for murders."

"I don't think that's the answer—"

"Did I ask your opinion?" Oliver sneered.

"You should. Your man is right, Oliver."

D'Agostini walked into the office, his voice grim but the steel of his eyes unbendable. "I'm surprised at you. I don't think you've ever let your emotions rule your decisions. Can't say I like this side of you, Oliver, but I guess it's understandable. Lomax has certainly gotten the best of you over the last few days, hasn't he?" His eyes took in the bloody features. "In more ways than one, it seems."

Oliver forced himself to sit back in his chair.

"I'm going to tell you what we're going to do," Richard said. "Instead of flushing them out and bringing more unnecessary attention to this problem, we're going to do what we should have done in the first place. We're going to bring them to us."

"And how do you propose to do that?" Kragen said with sarcasm. "Call them up for tea?"

Richard D'Agostini's features subtly took on a hard edge. "Oliver, I'll excuse the impertinent behavior, simply because I know you're not at your best. But make no mistake. While I've found your services and devotion exceptional in the past, I will not tolerate insubordination among my people. Do you understand me?"

"Yes," the aide agreed, but inside he seethed.

"I have arranged a meeting tonight. A very important meeting." Richard said. "One that will take care of Jacob Lomax. You just make sure you're here to greet the couple when they show. Understand me?"

"Yes."

"Now, I think you've had a long day, Oliver," Richard observed. "I want you to get a good night's sleep. I'll take Mr. Sweeney here for my meeting. He will inform you of what happens later."

Kragen fisted his hands. The senator was giving him a disciplinary slap by making him go through his own subordinate for information. Kragen looked at Frank, but the enforcer was smart enough to show no reaction over the change of plans.

"Of course," Oliver responded, his lips tight. "I'll be here, waiting."

Chapter Twenty

Pusher had made himself comfortable with a sandwich from room service. Although the man moved slowly and chewed even more slowly, Jacob was relieved he would suffer no permanent damage from his injuries.

Jacob showed the ex-con the paper from Grace's phone. "Try this."

Pusher took a look at the series of numbers. "It's not the right type of code for the USB. I don't know what this is for, but it's not the one I need."

"Is the thumb drive working?"

"So far so good. But I won't be really able to tell until I can access the information," Pusher explained. "How much time do I have to decrypt this?"

"Less than ten hours."

"I'll do my best."

Jacob arched an eyebrow.

"Ten it is."

Jacob placed a hand on the younger man's shoulder. "Thanks, Pusher."

"No problem." The younger man's smile went lopsided under the swelling. He winced and touched his lips. "Besides, I owe them a little back."

Grace walked up to the men. "Will we be safe here?"

"Yes," Jacob lied, knowing they wouldn't be safe until he finished this. "At least until tomorrow. The senator is going to be dealing with the aftermath of the commotion tonight."

"Why don't you two get some rest," Pusher suggested. "If you want me to crack this, I'm going to need some quality time alone."

Grace smiled. "Okay, Pusher. I need to talk to Jacob, anyway."

Jacob followed Grace into the bedroom. During the ride home, emotions and memories stampeded through him, leaving his inside battered, his mind overloaded.

"Do you think the fire alarm was a coincidence?"

"Maybe." But neither of them truly believed it.

Suddenly, he heard the click of the lock before she crossed the floor to him. "All I could think when we were running over the lawn was what would have happened if we'd been caught."

With a gentle hand, she pushed him until he sat on the bed. "And I knew what they had done to Pusher wouldn't have even been close to what Kragen would've done to you."

"Grace—"

"I saw Kragen's eyes, Jacob. That man wanted to tear you apart."

Jacob felt the flutter of her fingers across his forehead as she brushed his hair back, then kissed his wound. "Grace."

"I decided then, at that moment, what I wanted."

"And what's that?"

"You," she said softly. "For tonight, tomorrow. For as long as we can have."

"You mean, for as long as my amnesia lasts," Jacob corrected. "And when my memory returns?"

"We'll have a decision to make."

When she stepped closer, he cupped the small

of her back with his palms, brought her body in tight to his. "The baby is mine, isn't it?"

"Yes."

He had anticipated her answer. Still, his hands flexed against her in reaction.

"Jacob, I couldn't tell you before—"

Tears swelled in her caramel eyes, then spilled. He wiped the dampness with his thumb, tracing the bones of her cheek, the soft line of her jaw. "Shh. Tomorrow. We'll deal with it all tomorrow."

He studied her mouth, loving the soft curves, the slight tremble of anticipation.

"I've missed you," he murmured, then covered her lips with his own, catching the next quiver, soothing it with his tongue until she whimpered with pleasure.

His fingers moved to the back of her hair, releasing the pins, letting them drop—forgotten before they hit the floor.

The silky ends of her hair fell, then flowed over his hands.

One of them shuddered. He didn't know which one. He only knew he didn't care.

Her lips softened under his. She sighed, then shifted, trying to fit her body to his. He tasted the sweet curve of her shoulder while his fingers traced the bare skin of her back.

He caught her dress zipper between his thumb and forefinger and tugged, letting the side of his hand ride the bumps of her spine down to the small hollow above her hips.

"Wait," she murmured.

Slowly, he pulled back, but no more than a breath away. She reached up, took one end of his tie and slid it free. The silk whispered against his shirt in a long, seductive hiss. She dropped it to the ground.

Her fingers found the buttons of his shirt and slipped them free one by one. His heart picked up speed and he moved her hand to his bare chest. "See what you do to me, Grace?"

"What if I want to do more?" Loose, her dress slipped to the floor in a long, sexy sigh, leaving a puddle of chiffon at her feet.

She wore nothing now, except a wisp of white lace just under the round swell of her belly, a small scrap of material that provided no protection from his gaze. "How much more?" he rasped, as his eyes followed the long lean lines of her legs up to the gentle flare of her hips and back again to her belly.

A stab of possessiveness shot through him, on its heels a jolt of the need to protect her and his baby inside her.

"So much more," she murmured. She started to slip out of her heels, but a hand on her thigh, stopped her.

"Not yet."

Grace smiled, a wicked curve of the lips that thickened the blood in his veins.

Slowly, she stepped out of her dress, slid into his lap and straddled his waist. She guided his hand from the curve of her hip, down the length of her leg, stopping only when his palm flexed against the curve of her ankle and his fingers slipped under the strap of her sandal. "I never knew high heels turned you on."

Jacob shuddered, absorbing another punch of desire, before his hand gave in to the need to feel the silk of skin again. "I didn't, either," he admitted, while his fingers traveled back to her hip. "Let's find out what else I like."

His hand cupped the roundness of her belly—soft in tenderness, lingering with pos-sessiveness.

Then he jerked back, his eyes wide.

The baby bumped his hand again.

Grace would've paid good money to be able

to laugh. But the emotion caught at the back of her throat. She didn't think it was often that Jacob got caught off guard.

But he recovered quickly, she thought with delicious pleasure. His lips skimmed her shoulder, followed the delicate curve of her neck, tasted the hollow of her collarbone.

With a sigh, she leaned back. Just for a moment. Just for support. His mouth settled over one sensitive nipple, tugging, tasting. Little electric shocks exploded under his lips, setting her nerves humming.

He moved slowly, maddeningly so. Nibbling here, stroking there. She tugged off his shirt to show her impatience. When that didn't change his tempo, she fisted his hair, holding him still until her mouth found his. Hard, hot, impatient.

Suddenly, Grace was beneath him, the final barriers gone. The wisp of lace, torn and thrown. His pants peeled away and left beside her gown.

Jacob used his elbows for support, not wanting to crush the baby, but wanting—needing—it between them.

A double-edged sword of pain and pleasure sliced through skin, gut and bone. How could he have turned away from this, turned away from her?

He shifted back, bringing her hips to the edge of the bed. Her calves slid up over his shoulders. He absorbed the pleasure with the pain when one balanced over his wound.

His hands found the soft cheeks of her derriere. Because he could, he squeezed each, heard her gasp before he hitched her hips higher.

She felt open, exposed, balanced on the edge. Her heart beat, fluttering with fear. Of what, she didn't know. She gripped the covers in tight fists, trying to keep from falling.

At that moment, he slid into her.

They both groaned. "I'm a selfish bastard, honey, but I need to hear you say it."

Grace understood. His face was savage despite the endearment. The pain became unbearable, the words burned the back of her throat. Too much pain already, she thought. She looked into his eyes and stepped off the edge. "I love you, Jacob Lomax. I always have and I always will."

His muscles bunched reflexively against her, telling her what she needed to know.

The only way she needed to know.

He took her then, on a long, shuddered sigh—sweeping her into a rhythm that had her rising, cresting, tumbling into a free fall.

And for the first time in a long time, she wasn't afraid.

Chapter Twenty-One

I love you, Jacob Lomax.

Jacob watched Grace fall asleep in the crook of his arm. Lord, he hoped so. But even as she spoke the words, he understood they wouldn't get her through the next twenty-four hours.

The flashes of memories were coming at breakneck speed, tumbling over each other, battering the wall that had held them back for so long.

Jacob had parents, still living. Still together after almost forty years. Grace had been wrong. He had family, he had friends. No more than a handful, but friends he trusted.

He also had a past.

The memories of Helene remained just out of reach. But they were right there, lingering on the edge of the others. They would come soon, he knew. And then he'd be prepared.

Determined, he gathered Grace closer, closed his eyes and planned.

A SLIGHT TAP ON THE DOOR had Jacob up and out of bed. He reached for his gun on the nearby nightstand.

"Lomax." The bar manager let out a long, low whistle through the door. "We just opened Pandora's box."

Jacob opened the door, stepped through, then shut it quietly behind him. "Show me."

For the next hour, Jacob scanned the Primoris files. "Can this be copied?"

"With a little time," Pusher replied, concern deepening his accent. "I have to bypass more security codes."

"How long?"

"At least a few more hours," Pusher answered.

"We don't have a few hours." Jacob grabbed the USB from the side of the computer. Their escape from the party tonight had terrified him. Now that he understood what he was dealing with, he wasn't going to let her near the situation.

"I need you to watch over Grace." He handed Pusher his pistol. "See that door? No one gets through that door alive."

"Hey, man, my specialty is computers—" Pusher stopped. "Hell. All right. Why not."

"Thanks. I'll be back as soon as I can."

"She's going to want to know what happened to you."

"Tell her I'm taking care of some business,"

answered Jacob as he picked up the phone and punched in the number. When the other side clicked, he said. "It's me. I've got the files."

CHARLES RENNE PARKED his car in the parking garage on the west end of the city and waited.

When headlights flared in his back window, he opened the door and stepped out.

Sweeney approached him and quickly patted Charles down. "The senator would like to have a word with you, Doctor Renne."

Charles said nothing. Instead, he waited until Sweeney opened the limousine door.

When Charles slid onto the seat beside him, D'Agostini didn't bother with the usual pleasantries. "They showed up at the fund-raiser last night. They could have done serious damage to our plans."

"Who? Lomax?"

"With your daughter. They managed to

escape with Pusher Davis. I need to know where they took him."

"And I told you, I need time."

"You've had time, Charles. More than I've allowed anyone else. Now I am out of patience. The election machines are waiting to be shipped from the warehouse. I need that source code."

Anger rose in Charles, burning hot until it threatened to spew from every pore in his body. "If Sweeney hadn't showed up at Grace's house, I would've contacted you and taken care of everything myself. But your man Kragen had to send in his enforcer. He put everything at risk. Not me."

"That was unfortunate," the senator said. "But you had assured me from the beginning that your daughter would not be a complication when you told me about Helene's deception. And here she is right in the middle of the problem."

From the first time Charles had met Helene, there had been something vaguely familiar about her. But it was only a few days ago that he placed her as Langdon's daughter. She was the identical image of her mother.

"I need you to contact Grace."

"I told you, I can't find her."

"I have a hard time believing that, Charles. What I need you to do is persuade her to meet with you. And have her bring the Primoris files and the code."

"And how am I supposed to do that?"

"Tell her you're in danger," D'Agostini suggested.

"You really think she'll believe me?"

"Yes, because if she doesn't, your being in danger will be the truth."

Fear, dark and ugly, slithered beneath Charles's skin. "I will do whatever is necessary. After all these years, there should be no question of my loyalty. Didn't I warn you that Helene was an imposter? Didn't I tell you about her meeting with Lomax? Once Grace mentioned she'd be at the club that night—"

"Your loyalty was bought and paid for, so it's always in question. What I'm concerned about is your devotion to your daughter. Will it become an obstacle?"

"None whatsoever," Charles argued. "You forget, she's never been my daughter."

Chapter Twenty-Two

I've missed you.

The memory nudged Grace from hazy edges of sleep. But it was the actual words that had her sitting straight up in Jacob's bed.

A glance around the bedroom told her he'd left. He wouldn't desert her. She knew him too well now. But he'd certainly protect her.

Even if it meant breaking his promise.

She drew her knees up under the sheet, then rested her forehead against them. He was putting his life at risk to save her and their baby.

Grace got up and slipped on Jacob's robe, hugging it close.

The scent of coffee drifted through the open door.

Her heart jumped. She smiled, chiding herself.

She rushed down the stairs, not caring if she wore her heart on her sleeve. "I thought you'd left."

Pusher stepped out from the kitchen. "He did."

He handed her some tea. "He gave me his gun and told me to protect you."

"Protect me." She nodded. So she had been right.

The phone rang, startling her. She automatically reached for it. Only Jacob knew where they were.

Carol's number. Her father.

"Dad."

"No, Miss Renne. This is Oliver Kragen. We met last night."

"How did you get this number? What have you done to Carol?"

"We have not harmed your housekeeper. In fact, she probably hasn't even realized her phone is gone."

"Then how—"

"Your father. Of course, he gave it to us somewhat reluctantly. Which is one of the reasons I'm calling."

"You better not have harmed him—"

"Or what?" Kragen laughed, a savage sound that chilled Grace to the bone. "You're going to send Jacob Lomax after me? Why don't you put him on the phone. I'd rather cut out the middle man anyway."

"He's in the shower."

"Please, Miss Renne, don't play—" Kragan stopped. "He's not there, is he?"

She could hear him smiling over the phone. "Well, well. Is he out hunting up the bad men for you?" Kragen asked. "Seems the father of your baby is an undercover government operative. Independent contractor, actually, which is why it made it difficult for us to find out information on him."

"He's not the father—"

"Please. I told you, I have been talking to your father." Kragen chided. "Not that it's important. What's important is that I have someone here who needs to speak to you."

"Grace, it's me."

His voice was harsh, ragged. As if he had run a marathon or was in pain. "Dad."

"They want the input code and the Primoris files, Grace. Helene stole both from them. Don't give—"

Kragen came back on the line. "In fact, Miss Renne, we want it back so much, that we're willing to kill for it. Starting with your father here. Now I know you're alone, so this should be relatively easy. I'm going to give you very specific directions on where to meet my car in fifteen minutes. I'll be waiting. If you're a second late, you'll be an orphan."

"I won't be. Just tell me where to meet you."

"In front of the Library of Congress."

"How do I know to trust you?"

"You don't."

The phone went dead.

"No, Grace. Don't do this. Let Jacob handle this one. He'll save your father."

"Pusher, I need you to stay here in case Jacob comes back."

"The hell with that. If he comes back and finds you gone and me still here, I'm worse than dead. No thanks, I'll take my chances with that psycho Kragen again."

"No."

"Yes," Pusher insisted. "They think you're going in alone. I'll just tag along at a distance.

Watch your back until Jacob saves the day." He winked. "What do you think?"

KRAGEN PUSHED OPEN the double steel doors and motioned Grace in with his pistol. "The senator's waiting."

The warehouse smelled of cardboard and antiseptic. But, for a warehouse, it seemed unnaturally quiet. Only the squeak of her sneakers against cement echoed through the half-acre-large building.

Senator D'Agostini stepped out from behind a shelf filled with crates. "Were you followed, Oliver?"

"No. But we did pick up a hitchhiker." Miller stepped forward and shoved Pusher to the ground. "He tried to tail my car."

"Mr. Davis. This is a pleasant surprise," Richard said with a smile that didn't quite touch the cold, gray eyes.

"The pleasure's all mine."

"Really?" He nodded to Miller. The big man swung his foot, connecting hard with Pusher's ribs. The bar manager grunted, and rolled into a tight ball from the pain.

"Don't," Grace screamed and stepped forward.

"Shut up." Kragen jerked her back, his fingers digging hard into her skin.

"And Lomax?" Richard asked, his gaze on Grace. "Has he disappeared?"

"For now. But he'll show up soon enough once he realizes we have her." Kragen pulled Grace's phone from his pocket. "He'll call to check in and I'll make sure he knows where to find her."

"And Sweeney? Where is he?"

"Checking the perimeter with his men. I want to be ready when Lomax puts in an appearance."

"Well, let's get to it, then," Richard replied. "Do you have the code, Grace?"

"No. But I know where it is." She glanced at Pusher, caught the defiant anger in his eyes. "I can take you there, but first I want to see my father."

D'Agostini laughed. "You've watched too many movies, Grace." He walked over to Oliver and nodded toward his pistol. "May I?"

Before Grace could react, the gun exploded next to her ear. Pusher cried out, grabbing his shoulder. Blood seeped through his fingers.

"Pusher." Grace would've run forward, but Kragen grabbed her arm and jerked, sending her to her knees.

"Now, I will start putting a bullet in your friend each minute you wait. And trust me, it will take several before he dies from loss of blood."

"Don't, Gracie," Pusher ordered. "Trust me. You tell them, you're dead. I'm dead, anyway."

Miller reached down and squeezed Pusher's shoulder until the younger man cried out again from the pain.

"Do you think you can stand here and watch us take your friend apart, Grace?" Richard's lips thinned over his teeth in a feral smile. "You would be amazed at how much pain the human body can take when the bullets are well placed."

D'Agostini took aim at one of Pusher's knees.

"I don't have it, damn you!" Fear cramped her belly, bile rose to the back of her throat. "I was bluffing. I don't have the code or the key."

"Then you'd better hope, Miss Renne, that your lover does," D'Agostini said. "Miller. Find out where Sweeney is. Inform him to watch for Jacob Lomax. If Miss Renne doesn't have what we are looking for, Lomax does. If he has the code and key on his person, you may kill him. If he doesn't, I want him brought to me."

Chapter Twenty-Three

A platform of crates stood in front of the machine, still hooked to the chains that lifted it from a nearby storage pit in the floor.

For a moment, Frank Sweeney toyed with the idea of climbing the stack to get a good look from overhead, but quickly discarded the idea. If he got spotted, he'd put himself in a bad position.

Lomax was one canny son of a bitch. There was no doubt in the enforcer's mind that Lomax would show up sooner rather than later.

But that was fine with Frank. He was more than ready to get the show on the road.

A series of low grunts drifted from across the warehouse. On its heels came the echo of scuffling feet, the thud of a body slammed against a nearby wall.

Frank grabbed the gun from his shoulder holster and circled toward the sounds.

Suddenly, Miller stepped from behind some crates and grinned at Frank. He waved his gun toward Lomax, who knelt on the floor in front of the big man's feet. "Look what I found, boss."

"Good work." His eyes swept over Lomax, taking in the blood at his mouth, the look of disgust that hardened his features.

Frank raised his gun and fired. Miller grunted and fell to the floor dead, the back of his skull splattered the crates behind him.

"I've had it with you, Lomax. First you call

me out of the blue and tell me you're on your way here," Frank snapped. "Then you let that idiot catch you by surprise. How in the hell did that happen?"

"He just caught me and we'll leave it at that," Jacob snarled out and wiped his mouth with the back of his hand.

"So you decided to trust me and not run away this time?" Frank snagged Jacob's gun from Miller's hand and gave it back to his partner.

"I wouldn't have run away from you the last time except I didn't know who the hell you were." Jacob dropped the clip, checked it and shoved it back into the pistol.

"What the hell does that mean? If you're trying to pull some crap because I owe you a crack on your skull—"

"It's the truth. I had amnesia. I'll fill you in later." Quickly, Jacob scanned the warehouse. "I have the files and the code. And I've already called in the cavalry. They should be here anytime now."

Frank swore. "Jacob, they've got Grace. The moment this place fills up with agents, she's dead."

"I left Grace at the hotel—"

"She came here to save her father."

"What? Her father?" Jacob scowled. "Did she find him with D'Agostini?"

"No. And she's not going to handle finding out he's a traitor."

"I'll deal with that."

"Pusher Davis is with her. The man needs to stick to bartending. D'Agostini's using him for bullet practice to make Grace give up the Primoris files. I had to choose you or him. I'm hoping Grace keeps him alive. Hate to see him die, especially after I helped save his butt the other night. He took a hell of a beating before you showed your ass up to save the day."

"You set off the fire alarms."

"You're damn right I did." Frank grinned. "Felt good, too. Didn't like watching that Pusher kid take a beating." Frank cocked his gun. "Let's go save your lady friend before the troops get here."

"No. You go stop the troops and anyone else who gets in the way. I'll get to her and keep her safe until everything's clear."

"Okay, man. But watch your back. Kragen's with D'Agostini and that man is no pushover." Frank turned to leave, then stopped. He placed a hand on Jacob's good shoulder. Gave it a gentle squeeze. "About Helene. I didn't know they made her, Jacob. I would've gotten a warning to you somehow. Webber handled the hit—"

"It's okay, Frank. We all know the score. Helene more than anyone. Just bring our friends in quietly until I give you the all clear. It's time D'Agostini got his payback."

"You got it. And when we're done, I'm taking a vacation."

"Me, too," Jacob murmured as he watched Frank slip back into the shadows. "But mine's going to be a honeymoon."

"I wouldn't count on it, Lomax." Kragen stepped from behind a nearby crate, his pistol pointed at Jacob's chest.

"WHERE'S Sweeney?" Kragen took Jacob's gun and tossed it across the floor.

Jacob shrugged, using the movement to loosen the tight muscles between his shoulders. "Around."

"How long has he been working for you?"

"He works with me," Jacob mused. "And we work for the good guys."

"Was Helene Garrett just one of the *guys,* then?" Kragen snorted. "It doesn't matter. Within a month, we'll be the good guys as far as the nation is concerned."

When Jacob didn't respond, Kragen said, "They won't believe him, you know. Too many people involved with too many connections. Frank doesn't stand a chance of convincing anyone without the disk."

"What makes you think he doesn't have it?"

"The fact that your girlfriend is just past those doors with the senator. You need the disk to save her. Not that it will help. She's probably dead already."

Fear slithered up Jacob's spine, coiled in his chest.

"I don't want the disk as much as the senator. You see, my name isn't on it. I made sure of that."

"And Frank Sweeney?"

"Once I kill you, there will be no one to protect him."

When Jacob didn't respond, Kragen waved his gun. "We could use these and have our own version of the shootout at the O.K. Corral. Or we can have our own little Tuesday night takedown. What do you say?"

Keeping his gun drawn, Kragen slipped out of his suit jacket, folded it in half and laid it over the nearest crate.

"I'm willing, considering my disadvantage right now."

Kragen laughed and tossed his own gun by Jacob's. "Now we're on equal ground."

Lomax waved his fingers, crooking them at Kragen. "Let's get it done then, Oliver. Why waste time?"

"That's right, you have the girl to save."

Kragen rushed Jacob, backing him up with a flurry of kicks and punches. Jacob blocked most with his forearms and absorbed others with his upper body before he dove underneath and rolled. He came up into a roundhouse kick that connected with Kragen's jaw.

Kragen stumbled back two steps. He rubbed his jaw. "Not bad."

"Want more?"

Kragen charged Jacob again. At the last minute he pivoted, catching Jacob off guard. His heel slammed into Jacob's forehead. Razor sharp stars burst behind Jacob's eyes.

He caught Kragen's leg, came up to jam a knee in his groin. Kragen immediately collapsed his other leg, sending both men to the floor.

Both men rolled, grappling for a death hold. Jacob grabbed Kragen from behind, his forearm wedged under Kragen's neck, squeezing.

Choking, Kragen reached behind, grabbed Jacob's shoulder and gouged. White-hot pain shot through Jacob's arm and up his back, forcing him to let go of Kragen.

Kragen flipped away, but remained on the

floor. Both men blew the oxygen in and out of their lungs.

Blood trickled into Jacob's eye. He wiped it away with the back of his hand. "Come on," he growled, scrambling to his feet.

Kragen kicked, aiming for Jacob's wound again. Pain exploded, knocking the breath from him. But this time, Jacob was ready for the jolt. He staggered but stayed upright.

He heard it then, the sound of shots. Grace's scream.

With a savage cry, he fought past the pain, focusing his mind on the one obstacle between him and his family.

His family.

Jacob rammed Kragen in a football tackle, smashing them both into the crates on the nearby pallet. Oliver grunted, his hands grappling for a hold on Jacob's neck. "She's dead, Lomax. Can you feel it?"

Kragen forgot the neck and aimed a fist into Jacob's ribs, knocking himself free. "You think you can stop this? This is bigger than you or me. Bigger than the United States. We're talking world domination, Lomax. The most powerful men in the world have come together. World bankers, world leaders. Industrial giants. Do you really think you can stop that?"

"Maybe not, but I will stop you." Jacob got his feet under him. "Let's finish it."

Kragen moved, knocking Jacob back into the chains. Jacob grabbed hold of one chain for balance, kneed Kragen in the groin. Kragen fell backward onto the controls. Suddenly, the floor shifted beneath them.

Kragen tackled Jacob, rolling to the edge of the platform as they rose toward the warehouse rafters. His hands were around Jacob's neck squeezing the oxygen from his throat, forcing Jacob's head back. "Tell Helene hello from me when you see her."

Jacob's neck muscles corded, straining against Kragen's strength. At the last moment, he pivoted, bringing his good arm down on Kragen's hands, breaking the contact.

Jacob went to his knees. He wrapped his bad arm around a chain for balance as he heaved in bursts of oxygen.

Kragen charged, intending to knock Jacob off the platform.

Jacob grabbed Kragen's shirt and yanked, using the other man's momentum against his attack. The weight of both men flipped them off the platform. Jacob grunted in pain as the chain caught his bad arm, keeping him suspended midair.

"Go to hell," he rasped as he let go of Kragen's shirt.

Kragen screamed, his hands flying, grabbing

at air as he fell. His body dropped into the pit. Jacob heard it bounce, once…twice with sickening thumps before hitting the floor. Jacob dangled for a moment, while his eyes searched the floor beneath. Kragen's head lay at an unnatural angle, his sightless eyes open and gazing up.

With his good arm, he maneuvered himself back up on the platform and hit the button. As soon as he could, he jumped to the floor, snagged his gun and ran. His mind was repeating the only word he could think of. *Please. Please. Please.*

D'AGOSTINI PLACED HIS GUN at Grace's belly. "Just think if I fire now, I will be killing two birds with one bullet, don't you think?" A thin line of madness underlay the senator's laugh.

"Why don't you join us, Mr. Lomax? I'm

sure you'll want to hear what I have to say to the mother of your child."

Jacob approached, relief making his muscles shake. Grace was okay. Her cheek was bruised, her mouth was bleeding, but she was alive.

Pusher was another matter. The bar manager lay on the floor, bullet wounds in his shoulder and thigh.

"He's not dead yet. Only unconscious," Richard stated. "Like you, who should've died many times over. Maybe I should have hired you instead of trying to kill you."

"I'm particular about who I work for, Senator. Garbage, even the human kind, tends to come with a stench. One that I don't abide well."

Richard shrugged. "Charles Renne didn't seem to mind. Your father was easy to recruit, Grace."

"My father has nothing to do with this," she bit back.

"You are naive, aren't you? First your father, now your lover?"

"I have no idea what you're talking about."

"Betrayal. I'm talking about betrayal and how it does strange things to people.

"You see, once upon a time, your father suspected your mother was having an affair with Senator Langdon. So one night he drugged her. When he questioned her, she confessed everything.

"At the time, we suspected that Senator Langdon was gathering information on us. We had already decided he was a complication we needed to get rid of.

"What we didn't know was that your mother was privy to her lover's plans. She divulged many names, including mine. So when your father approached us, we took care of things for him."

"You caused the plane to crash?"

"I have to admit, he didn't expect us to kill your mother. But after, we convinced him that extreme actions are sometimes necessary. In this case, we saw his potential and needed something to guarantee his…loyalty.

"After her death it was easy enough to get him to drug others, gather intelligence. He was already involved. Neck deep, so to speak. When his reputation grew here in Washington, D.C., so did his role in our organization. He became our truth serum expert. Allows us to keep others loyal or destroy them. Whatever we deem fit."

"I don't believe you. My father couldn't hate my mother that much. Not to stand by and let her—"

"Die with her lover?" D'Agostini laughed. "How about once he found out that you weren't really his daughter? That the affair had been going on for quite a long time. How old were you when she died? Ten?"

When Grace didn't answer, he shrugged. "I guess once you were conceived, your biological parents parted ways. Seems when Senator Langdon failed to divorce his wife, your mom slept with Charles on the rebound. Up to your birth, she didn't know who the father was. But as the years passed, and she hadn't conceived any more children, it became apparent that Charles wasn't your father."

"And you're telling me that Langdon and my mother reconnected and that was the ultimate betrayal."

"Washington, D.C., is no more than a small town that loves to gossip. Whether they did or not, your father was being laughed at behind his back."

"I don't believe you."

"But you see, Grace, that isn't even the best

part of this story," D'Agostini taunted. "Senator Langdon had a family, too.

"A wife, who later committed suicide after falling into a depression." He paused. "And a daughter."

Grace froze, knowing what was coming. "Helene."

"And here I thought you weren't clever. Much quicker than I was, actually," he added ruefully. "Helene was a few years older than you at the time. Old enough to suspect the plane crash had been deliberate. You see, her father was an excellent pilot. She knew it because she spent many hours up there with him. Bonding time, I guess."

Was it true? She glanced at Jacob, saw the answer in his eyes. Grace locked her knees to keep her legs under her.

"She must have panicked when her sister fell in love with her partner and got pregnant."

Grace jerked with surprise.

"Oh yes, don't you think your dad would've told me? He told me so much more," D'Agostini mocked. He reached into his pocket and pulled out a recorder.

Grace heard her father's—no she corrected, Charles Renne's—voice. *"You forget. She was never my daughter in the first place."*

Everything inside her turned cold.

"Grace Ann." The whisper was harsh from behind her. She turned to see Charles step forward with a gun in his hand.

Jacob recognized it as Kragen's pistol.

"I said what I needed to keep D'Agostini from suspecting." Charles tilted the pistol up, pointing it at the senator. "It's over Richard," he added.

"It's a little late to play the hero now, isn't it, Charles?" Richard responded derisively. But Jacob noticed the senator kept his gun pointed at Grace's belly.

Jacob could feel the cold steel of his own 9 mm dig into the small of his back, but he couldn't take the risk.

"Let go of my daughter or I will shoot you."

"Shoot and I will kill your daughter. Oh wait, she's not your daughter," Richard said, snapping his fingers. "I keep forgetting."

"It's over, Senator. I have the code to the voting machines. I also have the files on your operation," Jacob said, his gaze flicking to Grace.

"And you think I won't get it from you?" The senator shook his head. "This is no mere operation, Lomax. An operation is run by two-bit criminals. Your small-mindedness is the reason you will fail."

"I haven't failed."

"You think what you have will bring Primoris to its knees?" His laugh was savage, the lines of his face distorted in his insanity.

"All it will do is set back our timetable for a decade, maybe two at the most. There will be others. Primoris is a global power. It goes far beyond the banks and governments. We control the militaries, the sciences, technologies, economies and the law, whether it's martial or otherwise. Do not kid yourself. We control the very air you breathe, the food you eat, the ground you walk on. And like sheep, you exist because of our benevolence," D'Agostini spouted, his voice raging at Jacob. "We are the elite, the one percent. We have no sympathy for the weak." Suddenly, the senator swung his gun toward Charles and fired.

Startled, Charles fired a split second later. His bullet hit D'Agostini directly in the heart. The senator looked down at the blood as it gathered on his chest and slowly sank to his knees. Looking at Charles with astonishment, he fell forward, dead.

Grace turned to her father just as he crumpled to the ground. Hurrying to him, she turned him over onto his back and saw that the bullet had entered his chest. Charles looked up at Grace and tried to speak, only to cough up blood.

"Dad." Tears flooded her eyes. She gathered him close into her lap. "Hold on, please!" she whispered urgently. "Call an ambulance!" She screamed the words at Jacob, but when he didn't move, she whispered, "Please."

"It's too late, Grace," her father rasped, while a deep, moist rattle shook his lungs.

"I love you." Tears formed in her eyes, causing his face to blur. Angrily, she wiped them away with the back of her hand. "You have to hold on. Everything will be fine but you have to hold on!"

Charles reached up and cupped Grace's

cheek in his hand, using his thumb to rub away a tear.

"Don't cry, honey. Not for me," he whispered. His hand dropped back to his chest. "It had to be this way, don't you see?" Blood bubbled at the corners of his mouth. "You're safe. That's all that matters."

"No, Daddy." Grace started crying in earnest now, her tears dripping unheeded onto her father's shirt. "Please, don't give up," she begged him. "Don't you dare die on me!"

Charles wrestled back another cough, but it cost him. "What I did to your mother, it was a mistake. I didn't…" He tried to inhale. "I love you…"

Grace shook her head, gripped him closer. "Don't. Don't, Dad. Stay with me."

But she knew Charles didn't hear her, didn't see her.

"Grace, I'm sor—" Jacob began.

"Don't say it. You remember, don't you?" she said dully, her eyes still on her father. Gently, she closed his eyes.

"Yes," Jacob answered, his tone flat with remorse.

"When?" She choked back the sob, the excruciating pain that sliced through her. Gently, she laid her father on the floor, then stood.

"Last night."

Her hands fisted before she could stop them. It took effort, but she forced them to relax. Anger wouldn't help, wouldn't make the facts any less harsh. "Before we—"

"Yes."

The word was a knife that severed an already damaged heart.

"Grace, its not—"

"Get away from me." She could've contained the rage, the slap of betrayal if he hadn't reached for her. Blindly, she struck at him when he tried to hold her. The second sob caught her off guard, then a sweep of them couldn't be stopped.

She cursed him, each word punctuated with the pounding of her fists against his chest. She didn't want to be touched, consoled. She wanted to grieve, to rage. She wanted to inflict the same pain that ripped her from chest to stomach.

Jacob took the hits, blocking them only when he thought she'd hurt herself. Eventually the screaming turned to guttural sobs, then desperate whimpers. Only then did he gather her close.

Drained, Grace couldn't, didn't resist. Minutes blurred together until Grace lost all sense of time.

Finally, when she gained some control, she moved away. "I'm okay now."

When he stepped to her again, she raised her hand. "Don't."

"Grace, we need to talk."

"You left me. You gave me your word. And at the first moment you had to make a decision on whether to be truthful, you left. I thought I understood why, that you wanted to protect me and the baby. But this—" She waved her hand toward her father. "You had no right to protect me from this." Her stomach hurt, the insides twisting painfully with the betrayal. "Leave me alone, Jacob."

"I wasn't about to let you get killed, damn it."

"And as you can see, your plan worked out well." With gentle fingers, she reached down and brushed the hair away from her father's forehead. "I'm safe."

His sharp intake of breath told her she'd hit home. But she was already beyond caring. What he'd done, no matter the reason, wasn't forgivable.

"Grace, let me explain."

"No." She placed a hand to her stomach, willing the pain to stop. "You could've explained everything last night before you left me, damn you. We were in this together."

"I work for the government. Helene was an operative. One of my contacts."

"I don't care—"

"Listen!" He talked over her, almost believing that if he got the words out, she would understand. Maybe forgive. "She and I were meeting the other night because of the code. The one in your phone. It's the code that accesses the voting machines. Officials click on certain numbers and letters hidden on the touch screen and they can flip the vote to whatever party they want to win."

"I told you I don't care now," she said dully. "Last night, I might have cared. It might have made a difference. But you're too late."

Emotion, hurt, love, longing shot through him, catching in his chest, catching him off guard. He stepped back, reeling as memories flooded. Pain-filled memories of the first time he'd left her.

"Grace. The senator was right. Primoris is worldwide. Helene managed to gather intelligence on over a hundred men and women working toward global domination. Prime ministers. Generals. Presidents."

"I told you, I don't—" A harder pain hit her this time, deep within her belly. She bent over, fighting against the next spasm.

"Grace!"

She realized the cramping hadn't been from fear or the pain of losing her father. She looked down, saw the blood spotting her pants.

"Jacob, the baby," she whispered, terrified.

But the next spasm hit on another wave of gut-wrenching pain. "No, please—"

Jacob caught her before she hit the floor in a dead faint.

Chapter Twenty-Four

Two weeks later.

Mount Hope Cemetery was no more than a spot of grass and a grove of trees meshed between high-rises and skyscrapers on the streets of Washington, D.C.

But its history had long been established before the first historical monument had been erected. Long before the first war, even the first church. And Jacob had no doubt the cemetery would stand long after the last structure crumbled with age.

Gravestones dotted the small, rolling knoll. The cemetery was certainly more eclectic than the famed Arlington, but no less loved, if the flowers adorning most graves were any indication.

The newest of the gravestones was small, but so pristinely white it almost hurt the eyes. It lay by two others, no bigger, no more worn, but matching in a sallow-gray marble.

With a sigh, Jacob laid the pink roses against the white marble.

"Helene loved roses. She would buy them from the street vendor for our office."

He'd heard her, of course. Long before she spoke. The scent of the honeysuckle hung in the air, had mingled with the roses.

"I remember," he said. "She preferred red, but for some reason…it didn't feel right."

His eyes swept over Grace from behind

mirrored sunglasses. He hadn't seen her since the hospital. The day her father died.

"Isn't it too soon to be up on your feet?"

The concern in his voice warmed her heart.

"No." She shook her head when what she really wanted to do was take his hand, touch his face. Reassure him. "The doctor gave me her approval.

"She said I was to avoid stress, among other things." Her hand slid over her stomach, more pronounced than ever under the V-neck sweater, the loose cotton pants. But she wasn't surprised after a week of rest and spoiling from Carol.

"What other things?"

"Sex. Mainly," she teased and almost smiled at the growl that rumbled deep in his chest.

"I'm joking, Jacob.

When he didn't answer, her tone grew serious. "The pain had been from the stress, not the baby. And the blood—" even now, she had a hard time saying the words "—had been my father's."

She stepped closer to Helene's grave. Saw her parents' nearby. It had been her decision to bury them together. One she didn't regret. "A whole family destroyed because of power."

"I wish I could say it will never happen again," Jacob answered. "But corruption goes hand in hand with money and power."

She turned to him then, curious. "You know, you never explained why Helene went into business with me."

"I haven't seen you."

"Yes, you haven't explained that, either."

"I wanted to give you time. To heal. To adjust." He glanced at her, his gaze sharp and watchful. "To work through the anger so when I did see you, I wouldn't have to worry about injuries."

"And Helene?"

"Helene had government access to your whole life profile. It didn't take her long to discover you were her half sister. I think she just couldn't walk away from an opportunity to get to know you better. That outweighed any risk she might have been taking. But when you got pregnant, it changed everything."

"Why?"

"She wanted your baby to have a father. A good father, like she never had."

"And I never had," she added solemnly. "That's ironic if you think about it. I didn't want you to know because I didn't want the baby to have a father like I had. Emotionally removed. And Helene was going to tell you because she wanted the baby to have a real father. One who could love the baby. Helene had more faith in you than I did."

"Helene had an advantage. She knew my family background. Something I couldn't share with you. Not at the time. Not without risking your life."

Even now, it could hurt. The fact that he'd shared his life, his past with another woman so easily—trusted her so completely as a friend. "And now?"

"Now," he said, drawing out the word until it became two syllables, "I'd like to know what you're doing here."

"Pusher said you had left the bar with a bouquet of flowers. This was a logical conclusion. He says you've bought a bouquet every day."

"Not every day, but most days. I miss her, Grace."

"Me, too." Tears pricked the back of her eyes. She wasn't ready to talk about them yet. "How's the bar going?"

"I didn't realize when Helene left me the bar, she left me Pusher, too." He sent her a sexy, sidelong glance. "I don't suppose you'd come back as my partner?"

"I'm going to be really busy soon." She patted the flutter in her stomach, took a deep breath to settle the flutter in her heart. "Don't have any plans other than to get plenty of rest at my father's house."

"You're staying, then?"

"For a while. My father's being hailed a hero. His reputation is still intact. The only ones who know the truth now are you, me, Frank and Pusher," she said. "So I know his secret is safe."

"It is."

"What about you? I figured you'd leave Pusher in charge and head off on another mission."

"I'm retiring, actually. And thanks to Helene, I have a legitimate business to manage."

"What about your properties?"

"I can still manage them, too," Jacob said.

"I'm staying at a hotel for right now, but I'm thinking about having the boathouse rebuilt. Make some improvements. Make it a real home."

"You mean, you're staying here for good?"

"I left that first time to complete some unfinished business. I had every intention of getting back with you after I helped Helene bring down Primoris. Long before I found out you were pregnant."

She looked at him, startled.

"Helene told me the night she died. About you. About the baby. About the fact that she had to pass the information off to you. It frightened her, putting you in jeopardy like that, but she had no choice at the time. She had moved into the boathouse as an added precaution, but still suspected her cover had been blown. She thought someone had followed her to your lunch date. That's why she made the switch. When we were ambushed, I was on my way to you. The bullet that hit my shoulder went through me and caught Helene in the chest. She used her last breath to tell me she loved you."

Tears backed up in her throat. "I loved her, too. She was a sister to me in so many ways. I just never realized it until she was gone but she was my family."

"And Charles?"

"I still love him," Grace admitted. "He will always be my father. I haven't sorted it all out in my mind yet—or my heart—but I'm sure I will eventually."

"I guess that's it, then," Jacob said, his eyes resting for a last time on Helene's grave. "So you've told me how you found me, but you never told me why you came out here."

"We're having a baby girl. I found out this morning."

"We are?" The muscle in his jaw clenched and unclenched. "Grace, I don't have a right to ask your forgiveness—"

"Neither do I. But I'm going to ask you anyway. Will you forgive me, Jacob?"

"Forgive you?"

"What I said to you when my father died—"

"Was deserved." Jacob gathered her into his arms and kissed her softly. "I love you, Grace."

"I love you, too."

He hugged her to him for a moment, then pulled back. "I thought you wanted to be surprised with the baby's sex?"

She laughed. "I've had enough surprises for a while."

"Do you think you can handle one more?"

Her eyebrow rose, suspicious. "Depends on the kind of surprise."

"My dad is retired military. He and my mother own a bed-and-breakfast in Maine. I want you to meet my parents, Grace. I want you to look at my baby albums, see my old tree fort." Jacob buried his face in her neck, inhaled the sweet scent of honeysuckle. "While my parents are out playing bridge, I want to make love to you in my old bed, like a horny teenager. Then later whisper all my hopes and plans for our baby girl against your belly."

Love tightened her chest, squeezed a shimmer of tears from her eyes. Jacob was giving her more than his love, more than his trust. He was showing her his vulnerability. A precious gift from a man with so much control.

"I like Maine." Her arms circled his neck and for a minute she leaned into him, letting their hearts beat against each other. "But I don't go anywhere with strange men."

"Strange?"

Stiffening, he tried to pull away, only to

relax when she chuckled, tickling the base of his throat.

"Frank told me Lomax wasn't your real name."

"He did? When did he tell you that?"

"When he called for my chocolate chip cookie recipe," she replied. "He's the friend you have that likes to cook, huh?"

"Yes, he is," Jacob admitted. "He's also my partner. And my uncle."

"Your what?"

"My uncle. He's the one that got me into government work, much to my mother's dismay. He's her younger brother."

"And you hit him on the head?" She gasped. "No wonder he looked so shocked when you walked through my bedroom door."

"Shocked is putting it mildly. I guess for a moment he was relieved, until I didn't lower the gun. That's why he grabbed for you. He knew he could buy some time using you as a bargaining chip until he could figure out what the hell was going on. I think at one point, he assumed your dad had used some kind of brainwashing drugs on me."

"You hit him really hard, Jacob." Her brow lifted. "He's not going to forgive you anytime soon, is he?"

"I'm already forgiven."

"That easily?"

"Hell, no. I didn't say it was easy," Jacob growled. "I had to give him my boat."

Grace laughed. She had a feeling Frank was going to be one of her favorite people. "So, Lomax, what is your real last name? Frank wouldn't tell me."

"Alexander."

"Jacob Alexander," she murmured, nodding. "I like it."

"Me, too," he joked. Then picked her up and twirled her in a circle. "But I like Grace Alexander more."

Epilogue

Four months later

Grace watched Jacob hold his daughter. The two-day-old lay comfortably in the cradle of her daddy's arm, her belly full, her eyes half-closed with sleep.

Jacob sat next to her on the bed, near enough for Grace to rest her head on his shoulder.

"You're asking for trouble if you go ahead with this," Grace insisted. But Jacob wasn't listening. He was too preoccupied with the baby.

"I can't get over how thick her hair is," he

whispered, running light fingers over the honey-brown locks, then tickled a tiny ear before brushing across the delicate cheek. "And how small she was. Remember?"

"Yes, she still is." And Grace was remembering other things. The slight shake of his hand when he held his daughter for the first time. The way his jaw clenched and unclenched to fight the emotion that overwhelmed him. The first time he kissed her small forehead, and held them both in his arms together.

Tears pricked at the back of her eyes, shuddered deep in her chest.

"Now, what were you saying about trouble?"

"You know exactly what I am saying. What you're planning on doing is worse than tempting fate, Jacob," Grace admonished, but the temper was no longer there. If anyone could take on fate and win, it was Jacob Alexander.

"I don't have the faintest idea what you're

talking about, do you, honey?" he stage-whispered to their daughter, who was busy staring into the identical blue eyes of her father.

She bit her lip to keep the smile from getting the best of her. "You're spitting right in its face, and don't think I won't say 'I told you so'—"

"It's perfect. And you know that as well as I do." He held out his finger, smiling with pride when the baby grabbed it with her hand. "She's perfect."

How could you argue with a man who was driven by love?

A nurse walked in the door. The woman was young, with a short, bouncy bob of red hair and bottle-green eyes that took in Jacob in one long, feminine sweep.

"Are you ready for me to take her, Mr. Alexander?"

Grace glanced from father to daughter and felt her own heart quickening. "Not just yet," she answered for Jacob.

"All right. Call me if you need anything."

"I will. Thank you." The nurse started to leave, only to stop by the door. "By the way, the doctor wanted to know if you've decided on a name for your baby girl?"

Jacob glanced at his wife.

Grace didn't bother sighing. Instead, she took a deep breath, thought of her mother and waited for the ground to tremble. "All right," she agreed, resignedly. "But don't say I didn't warn you."

Jacob laughed and turned to the nurse. "Serenity. We're naming her Serenity."

* * * * *

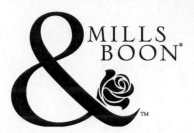